Thomas Westcott, God's Shadow Agent

Fictional Missions of the Christian Underground

The Martyrs' Friends Series

Book 1

Thomas Westcott, God's Shadow Agent

Fictional Missions of the Christian Underground

By

Alan W. Harris

Fruitful Tree Publishing
Luray, Virginia 22835

This book is published by:

Fruitful Tree Publishing

321 Camelot Court
Luray, Virginia 22835

www.StoriesChangeHearts.com

ISBN-13: 978-1-7341845-7-0

1. Harris, Alan W. 2. Christian 3. Fiction 4. Adventure 5. Teen 6. Young Adult 7. Character Development 8. Faith Building 9. Inspirational

This book is dedicated to all those who face loss, heartache, pain, and death in order to follow the Lord Jesus Christ.

"God of all Comfort, remember their blood and their tears. Pour out Your grace upon them, giving them the strength to stay faithful to you during their trials."

CONTENTS

PREFACE

I cannot imagine what life would be like without good stories. The gift of being able to tell a good story I believe comes from God. The reason I believe that is because God and His Son Jesus use stories so often in the Bible. An interesting tale well told can change a person's life and soften a hard heart. I've heard it said that the person who tells the best stories changes the culture. If that's true then we in this country are in desperate need for some really good ones. For a number of years I have been asking the Lord to direct me to write adventures that would draw people's hearts to Him. I have been faithful to record what I believe He has given me. It is up to my readers to decide their benefit.

There is more persecution against believers in Jesus Christ occurring right now around the world than at any other time in human history. The writer of the book of Hebrews in chapter thirteen verse three said, *"Remember the prisoners, as though in prison with them, and those who are ill-treated, since you yourselves are in the body."* As I prayed to God asking Him what story He wanted me to tell, I was strongly moved to write about those who suffer for the name of Jesus Christ, as well as the courageous believers who risk their lives to bring comfort and hope to the persecuted.

In order to help the reader feel more a part of the story, I decided to write it as if we have lost our freedoms, and are experiencing the same persecutions here today. Would we have the courage of our suffering brothers and sisters in other places? Would we have the willingness to risk our lives to help those who endure abuse for the name of Jesus but cannot help themselves?

Those are interesting questions, and we will never know the answer to them unless we experience persecution in our own lives. It is my prayer that if we are called to suffer for the name of Jesus that we would receive God's grace to be faithful and courageous for Christ like Thomas, Grace, Egg, and the others in this story. I also hope that as you read this exciting tale, each person is moved to follow our Lord and Savior more intensely than ever before.

And because I believe that good stories change hearts I have made sure that each chapter has opportunities for parents and teachers to use the chapter questions in Appendix A in order to teach important scriptural and character lessons to your listeners and readers. It is my hope that you will avail yourself of this resource since lessons taught while using an exciting story are lessons that go straight into long term memory. If you are interested in finding out about how this works, you can read more information regarding these documented and proven teaching principles at *StoriesChangeHearts.com*. Think about it. What would a parent or teacher give to know that the lessons that they teach will stay with their children or students for the rest of their lives?

Before I end, I want to thank my wonderful wife, Valerie for all of her help with editing and suggestions, without which the book would not be readable.

May God's richest blessings be granted to each of you!

Alan W. Harris
Luray, Virginia,
February 1, 2024

Chapter One

"*GREAT HONKIN' GEESE!*" the old man grumbled angrily as he swept the sidewalk in front of his rundown apartment building. *This used to be a nice neighborhood,* he thought, *but nobody cares anymore. You try to keep it clean, and the next day there's more trash than the day before.*

"OTHER PEOPLE LIVE HERE TOO, YOU KNOW!" the irritated elder shouted at no one in particular.

Suddenly the distracted man heard running behind him. As he turned, he was terrified to see a long-haired young man with a thin, scraggly beard sprinting straight for him. Before the elderly gentleman had time to dodge, the runner leaped over the old sweeper, performing a front flip, and landing in perfect stride as he continued to dash down the street.

Just as the stunned older man was grasping what had happened, two more running youths flipped over him and rushed after the first.

When the man realized that he was unhurt by the frightening ordeal, he sputtered his fury at the

1

hooligans as they raced away, shaking his broom threateningly.

The first runner led his two pursuers down the sidewalk, dodging pedestrians and flipping over railings. The leader leaped for a pole holding a sign advertising a law office that was protruding up from the edge of the sidewalk. Grasping the metal post, he swung rapidly around it and flung himself against the corner of the brick building. Almost miraculously, his strong fingers caught hold of the mortar joints of the bricks about ten feet up, and using his fingertips and the edges of his shoes, he rapidly climbed the corner of the building. Leaping up and out, he snatched the lip of a foot-wide ledge at the bottom of the third floor. In one move he drew himself on top of the shelf and, without a pause, leaped the narrow alley below, grabbing a windowsill on the next building. With a powerful grip and strong arms, the youth pulled himself with little effort onto the sill and immediately leapt up with a twist. He grabbed the overhang of the roof with both hands as he faced away from the building. He only hung there a brief moment before pulling his feet and legs up and over his hands and landing chest first on the flat roof.

The young man lay there, huffing to catch his breath, as he waited for his friends to join him. He was actually hoping the hard work out would help him calm down and get rid of some of his anger, but it hadn't.

Chapter One

A minute and a half later, the first of his two companions pulled himself over the edge of the building where he too collapsed on the roof gasping for breath. Another forty seconds passed before their third buddy's head appeared over the roof's edge.

"Help!" he grunted as his strength began to give out. Quickly, his two anxious friends hurriedly crawled to the ledge and, grabbing his arms, hauled him up to join them.

While their red-faced, exhausted friend lay beside them, repeatedly sucking in one lungful of air after another, the leader stood over him and shook his head in disappointment. "Beans, that was a pretty weak effort. You and Garrett need to work out more."

"You got to be kidding me!" Beans gasped. "That's the hardest thing we've ever done!"

"You've got to push yourselves if you want to improve," Mike declared with a hard face as he addressed both of his students.

While Beans continued to struggle to get air, Garrett answered their taunting friend. "We're at it every day, Mike; but you're such a superman, you can't relate to us normal people."

Beans lifted himself up on his elbow and huffed, "Mike, I've never even *heard* of anyone who can parkour like you! You're scary, man!"

Mike gave a brief smile at his friend's admiration but quickly changed the subject. "Well, it looks to me like that's all I'm gonna' get out of you two for this workout. You guys have had it," Mike announced, studying his exhausted friends. "We'll end the chase for today and let you guys recover."

"Okay," Garrett said, still breathing hard as he helped Beans rise to his feet. "We'll try it again next week. I'm okay with a challenge, Mike, but next time don't push it quite so hard. It's no fun if you think you're gonna' die because your grip is giving out.

"I gotta go."

"Okay, okay. Just work on your hand and arm strength," Mike advised as his friend headed to the edge of the building where the fire escape ladder was.

"See ya, Garrett!" Beans called as he sat down on the roof ledge next to his athletic friend.

"So what's goin' on, Mike?" Beans asked seriously.

"What do you mean?"

"You know Garrett and I are no match for you," his red-faced friend answered, still trying to catch his breath. "You never push our chases this hard. Something's eating you. What is it?"

For the briefest moment Mike stared at his friend, then he gave a deep sigh and put his head in his hands. After a long moment of thought, he finally answered, "I had this big blow out with my folks today."

"WHAT?!" Beans exclaimed in shocked disbelief. "Your parents yelled at you? I know your parents! They NEVER yell at you!"

"No, they didn't yell at me," Mike answered sheepishly. He gave a sigh and added, "Okay, to be honest, I'm the one who had the blow out. I yelled at them."

"Why?"

Mike looked around just to make sure no one could hear what he was about to say. "Because they won't cool it with all their religious stuff!"

"They're Christians, right?" Beans asked. "I've thought they might be. With all the junk the government's doin', a Christian is a pretty dangerous thing to be right now."

"You're tellin' me!" Mike shot back. "When I came in from work today, I heard my parents talking about how a number of their Christian friends had been arrested last night. They said that the police came and took a whole family…kids and everybody, and nobody knows where they are! Beans, that was just a few blocks from where I live!

"When I heard about it, I flipped out! I burst in on their conversation and demanded that they stop all their religious junk. I told them that I didn't want to go to prison because of their stupid beliefs. I guess I yelled that last part."

"What did your parents say?"

"The same thing they always say," Mike shot back. "They started telling me how much Jesus loves me, and how important He is to them…blah, blah, blah."

"So you got upset?" Beans prompted.

"I was scared…and mad, and I cut 'em off. I screamed at them again to just stop. My dad said that because of what Jesus had done for them, they couldn't quit serving Him. Then they started pulling out Bibles from a hidden place in the closet to take to other Christians. That's when I really lost it and left."

"What *has* Jesus done for them?" Beans asked curiously.

"He made them stupid! That's what He's done!" the angry youth shot back.

"What're you gonna' do?"

"What CAN I do, Beans? It's their lives! I've tried to make them understand what all of this is doing to me, but they won't stop!"

"Well, one thing's for sure," his friend advised. "As long as they intend to be so active in their beliefs, then you should have a plan. You ought to keep a bag packed that you can grab if you need to run, and you should figure out where you can go if your family gets raided. Those secret police dudes are rough!"

"I know. I know!" Mike moaned."

"And one more thing," Beans added, putting his hand on his friend's shoulder, "if something bad happens, you need to be ready to run like only you can."

Chapter Two

Mike was in no hurry to face his parents again, so he took the long way home. The sun had set when he rounded the corner of the block where his family's apartment was. The crowd of people in front of his building caused him to freeze. Fear detonated in his stomach when he saw the uniformed police marching out the front door, dragging his parents. He watched his father jerk back and protest the physical abuse to an agent in a dark suit. The man was in his thirties and had a sharp nose and a black goatee. Without any expression, the agent slammed the back of his hand hard into the side of Mike's father's face.

"DAD...MOM...," but Mike's cry of anguish was cut off when his arm was suddenly grabbed, jerking him sideways.

"Quiet, Michael!" a voice hissed urgently in his ear as he was pulled away from the noisy crowd.

Mike turned and saw a familiar face. "Aunt Faye," he cried when he saw their grey-haired family friend, "the police are taking Mom and Dad!"

"Yes," came the firm, whispered response, "and they'll take you too if you don't be quiet and come with me!"

"But…"

"There is nothing we can do for your parents right now!" Faye answered firmly. "The police will be looking for their son, so we must get you out of sight until we can make some plans. Now come on! You're too big for me to drag!"

Seeing the wisdom in Faye's words, Mike pulled the hood of his sweatshirt over his head and took one more look at the black cars, the police, and the weasel-faced man dragging his parents away. In that instant he realized that he was watching the end of his life as he knew it, and it absolutely crushed him. It grieved him deeply to remember the harsh words he had last spoken to his parents.

Turning his back to the heart-wrenching scene, he followed the older woman to her apartment. With all the excitement on the street and the government agents questioning those in the crowd, no one paid any attention to a hooded man assisting an older woman down the street. They walked the two-block trip to Faye's apartment building without mishap. Making sure they weren't being followed, Faye led them into the building and up the stairs.

Once inside her home, the older woman quickly locked the door and closed the blinds. Mike dropped, trembling, on her couch and sobbed, both in anguish and in anger.

"Your mother asked me to look out for you if something like this happened to them," Faye said.

"She asked you?!" Mike said in shock. "That sounds like she expected this!"

"Of course, they expected it."

"THEN WHY DIDN'T THEY STOP?!"

"Michael," Faye returned with a shocked expression of her own, "your parents are not fake believers! They are the real thing, and Jesus means the world to them! They can't stop serving Him!"

Michael sat in distraught silence for a moment, then said, "What am I gonna' do, Aunt Faye? The police have my parents! I've got nobody and no place to go!"

"Don't worry about that. I have some friends who can help us figure out what to do. For now, you'll have to stay here, and keep out of sight."

Faye could tell Mike was worn out physically and emotionally, so she heated a bowl of soup left over from her lunch. While he was eating, she made a bed for him on her couch.

"When you finish, Michael, lie down and try to rest. Tomorrow I'll go out and meet with my friends."

After he drained the bowl of soup, Mike tried to sleep, but he was still too upset. Through the partially open door to Faye's bedroom, Mike saw the older woman on her knees beside her bed, having a very passionate conversation with her Lord.

A gentle hand on his shoulder woke Mike from troubled dreams. Sunlight was streaming through the edges of the closed window blinds.

"Michael," Faye said as she looked down on him, "I'm going to the store, and while I am out I will talk with those folks who can help us. So don't you worry, and don't go outside or stand in the windows. I'll be back in a couple of hours."

It was all he could do not to take a peek to see if the police were still looking for him. He tried to follow Bean's advice to think through his situation and come up with a plan, but the whole situation overwhelmed him. He had nothing, and he needed help...lots of it, but he didn't know who he could trust. Maybe he could trust Beans, but then he realized that, if the police threatened Beans or his family, Michael's friend would do what anybody else would do. He would tell the police all he knew.

Michael considered that maybe he could try to sneak out of town at night, but where would he go? How would he live? Where could he make money and get food? He finally decided, if Aunt Faye and her friends couldn't help him, his situation was hopeless.

It was closer to three hours before Faye returned carrying a couple of shopping bags. "Michael," Faye called in a low voice as she placed her bags on the table, "I need you to come over here. We have a lot of work to do."

"Did you talk to your friends?" Mike asked hopefully.

"I did, but there are some concerns."

"What is it?" Mike asked with an anxious look. "What are *they* worried about? *I'm* the one the police are after! It's *my* life that's in danger here…not theirs!"

"Michael, calm down," Faye said firmly. "They will be putting themselves and their families in danger if they help you, and their concerns are legitimate. Because you aren't a believer in Jesus, the ones who could help you are concerned that you might turn them in to save yourself."

"No! No, I…I wouldn't! I…"

"Michael, anyone who is not prepared to face torture or death would say whatever they had to in order to escape that, and no one would blame them. It is because of your godly parents that my friends are going to help you, but they must do it in a way that protects them and their families."

"Okay…okay! I understand!" Mike returned anxiously, relieved that help would be coming. "What do I need to do?"

"Well," Fay began as she unloaded her bags, "first of all, we have to think of a new name for you. You're going to need to become a totally different person. After that, we'll give you a new look."

"A new name?" Mike asked with a confused expression on his face. "Uh…well…how about Robert?"

"Is there anyone in your family named that?" Faye asked.

"Yeah, my grandfather."

"Then it won't work," Faye shot back. "The police have unlimited resources and already know everything about you, your family, and your friends. It's got to be something totally unconnected with you. Could I make a suggestion?"

"Sure."

"How about Thomas?" Faye asked with a smile. "That was the name my husband and I picked out for our son who died at birth many years ago. I've always thought of you as a son."

"I'd be proud to be named Thomas," Mike said as he came over and put his arm around the older woman who was doing so much for him. "Could I take your last name?"

"Better not," Faye returned. "I'm sure they'll eventually figure out that I'm a friend of your family. That's why we need to get you out of here as soon as possible. Hey, how about Westcott as a last name? That was where my husband and I lived when we became believers."

"Thomas Westcott," Mike said the name out loud. "I like the way that sounds."

"Okay, Thomas, we got that out of the way," Faye responded. "Now we have to make Michael Morrison look like Thomas Westcott."

"What does Thomas Westcott look like?" Thomas asked with a smile.

"He looks different than you do," Fay returned seriously, "…a lot different."

Chapter Three

It was hard for him to watch his long, wavy hair drop into his lap as Faye trimmed it away.

"Can you leave it long enough to cover my ears?"

"I'm sorry, Mi...uh, Thomas," Faye returned, "but you can't look anything like the old Michael. I thought about shaving your head, but that might call too much attention to you. I'll leave you a little hair."

"Oh, my goodness!" Thomas gasped when he looked in the mirror. "I look so weird with short hair."

"I was going for *different*," Faye answered, "but I'll settle for weird if it saves your life."

"Okay," Thomas sighed with resignation, "now what?"

Suddenly a razor and a can of shaving cream was shoved in his face.

"I can't shave!"

"Why not?"

"I don't know how! I've never shaved in my life!"

15

"You'll figure it out," the older woman returned with a smile. "Before you use the razor, trim what you can with the scissors. Soak your face with warm water first before you put on the shaving cream. Then go slowly with the razor, and rinse it out often."

Thirty minutes later Thomas again studied himself in the mirror. "I...I look like a kid!"

"You haven't always acted like it," Faye returned, "but you're actually a young man. You're what...twenty years old now?"

"I'll be twenty-one next week," Thomas returned.

"Twenty-one, huh?" Faye said considering his looks. "I agree that the shave and haircut make you look younger. Maybe it will be enough to fool the police."

"Well, I sure do look a whole lot more kiddish than I did. So what do we do now?"

Faye looked at the clock. "We've got about forty minutes before my friends arrive. Let's clean everything up, then I'll fix us an early lunch."

It was just before noon when they heard a soft knock at the door. Thomas hid in the back bedroom near the window as Faye answered the door. Soon he heard the older woman's voice calling him.

Two men stood in the living room, each holding a cardboard box full of groceries. As they set the boxes on the dining table, Thomas noticed that they both wore dark blue overalls with the name 'Phillips Delivery' stenciled on the left pocket. They also wore matching blue caps and sunglasses. The older one had a short beard.

"Gentlemen," Faye announced, "this is Thomas Westcott."

As Thomas nodded to acknowledge the introduction, the younger of the two men began taking off his shoes and his overalls.

"Thomas," the older man said, "you'll need to put on his clothes. You're taking his place. When we walk out of here, you're going to be my employee in my delivery business."

"Is all this really necessary?" Thomas questioned when he was handed the overalls.

"There are police and detectives searching the streets below us. They're going in all of the apartments.

"They'll be coming here soon," he said, addressing Faye. "Go back over everything and make sure you get rid of any trace of Thomas's being here."

"I'll help you," the younger man said with a smile.

When Thomas was wearing the overalls and had replaced his shoes, the younger man handed him his sunglasses and cap.

"I hope we don't get stopped," the older man said, "but if we do, you work for me delivering packages, and we've got a lot more deliveries to make. Got it?"

"Uh...yeah, I think so."

"Okay, I want you to do something else before we walk out." The man pulled a small piece of plastic wrap out of his pocket and handed it to Thomas. "Inside this is some wax. Roll it up and shove it under your upper lip. It'll make your face look different."

"Thomas," Fay called.

The young man turned to face his family friend. As he did so, she threw her arms around his neck and hugged him tightly. "I don't know if we'll ever see each other again," she said in his ear, "but I want you to know that I love you and your family more than I can say. Your parents are the finest people I have ever known. I'm praying that you'll get to see them again, but if not, never forget that they love you. And as much as they love you, Jesus loves you more."

"Uh…thanks, Aunt Faye!" Thomas choked out as tears filled his eyes. "Thanks for everything!"

"We've got to go," the older man said, placing a hand on the young man's shoulder.

Suddenly Thomas found himself hurrying down the flights of steps, wishing that he had said something more meaningful to that sweet older lady who had risked so much for him.

When they reached the street, Thomas was surprised at all the activity. "Hurry! This way!" the older man called and led him toward his delivery truck. "Get in the blue van."

Thomas spotted the vehicle with *Philips Delivery* printed on the side and hurried to the passenger side door.

"Hey, you! Hold up! I want to talk to you."

Thomas turned to face the speaker. He saw a hard-faced man in a dark suit holding up a badge, looking suspiciously at him.

"Take off the hat and glasses," he ordered. "I want to get a look at you."

Thomas did as he was told, hoping that the wax under his lip was doing its job.

"What's your name?" the detective demanded.

"Mm…uh…T-Thomas…Thomas Westcott."

"You live around here?" he barked as he closely studied Thomas's face.

"I…um…I'm here making deliveries."

"Hmm…you seem nervous."

Thomas began looking for a way of escape.

"KID, I TOLD YOU TO GET IN THE VAN! WE'RE LATE! WHAT DO YOU THINK YOU'RE DOING?" Looking at the source of the yelling, Thomas and the detective saw the older man storming angrily around the van, glaring at them.

"I…I got stopped! This guy started asking me questions!"

Now the angry man's face turned towards the detective who was again holding up his badge. "Is that so? Well, this kid knows nothin'. It's his first day on the job. But if he don't quit draggin' his feet, it's gonna' be his LAST day!

"Listen, pal, we got a bunch more deliveries, and YOU are makin' us LATE!" As he said this, the older man shoved his clipboard with his delivery papers in front of the detective's face and pointed to the next delivery he had to make. "SO, ARE WE DONE HERE?"

The detective was taken aback and didn't know how to respond to the pushy delivery man, who took the policeman's silence as an answer to his question.

"GET IN THE VAN!" he barked at Thomas, smacking him on the back of the head to speed him up. "WE'RE LATE!"

Before the detective could stop them, Thomas and the driver jumped into the truck and raced away.

Chapter Four

As they drove off in the blue van, Thomas exhaled a chest full of air and exclaimed, "Whew, I thought sure he had me! I'm glad you said something when you did because I was getting ready to run!"

"It's a good thing you didn't," the driver answered. "Did you see all the police on that street? You'd have never made it."

"Maybe," Thomas returned, "but you've never seen me run. By the way, thank you…uh…I don't know your name."

"That's intentional," the man responded. "The only name you'll ever get from any of us is John Smith. Uh oh!"

"What is it?" Thomas asked with concern.

"Look up ahead," the driver answered. "There's a police check point. It looks like you're really important to them.

"Thomas, unbuckle your seat belt and crawl into the back of the van. Both of our lives depend on you doing exactly as I say."

Thomas instantly obeyed.

A few moments later, the van pulled up to the roadblock. "What's goin' on, Officer?" the driver asked through the open window.

"None of your business!" the armed trooper snarled back. "Get out of the vehicle! We're searching it!"

"Aw, have a heart, Officer!" the driver whined. "I've got a bunch of packages to deliver, and I'm way behind schedule."

"Then you better hurry up!" the trooper snapped. "Open up the back NOW!"

The driver climbed out of the van and walked to the back, accompanied by two of the troopers. The policemen pointed their weapons at the rear door as one of them said, "Open it up!"

When the interior was exposed, they saw a number of boxes and packages scattered around the floor, and dollies, ropes, and tools hung from the van walls. One of the officers leaned in and began shoving packages around, searching underneath.

"Be careful, will ya'?" the driver pleaded. "Some of that stuff can break!"

"Clear!" the trooper finally announced.

"Check underneath?" the first officer questioned as he kept his gun leveled at the driver.

With a growl of frustration, the second trooper dropped to a knee and scanned the underside of the van. "Nothin'!" he finally announced.

"Alright," the first officer snapped in an annoyed tone of voice, "get in the truck and get out of here!"

"If you broke anything, you guys are gonna' hear from me!" the driver barked as he hurried back to the driver's seat.

"Yeah, yeah…whatever," the officer growled.

As the van pulled away from the check point, the driver said, "All clear, Thomas. There's a latch behind your head. Pull it to unlock the door."

John Smith heard a click, and what appeared to be a stack of tools bungie-corded to the back corner suddenly swung outward, revealing a hidden space big enough to conceal a person. Thomas was red-faced and sweating profusely when he climbed out of the stifling secret cabinet.

"You okay?" the driver called back over his shoulder.

"Yeah, I guess," Thomas answered. "That was not pleasant."

"No, it's not," came the response, "but it saved you. Climb back up here in the seat."

In a few moments Thomas was up front, buckling his seat belt.

"Now, Thomas," the driver announced, "there's a black cloth bag by your feet. I want you to scoot your seat back, put that bag over your head, and lay your head on your knees."

"Why?" Thomas asked in confusion.

"It's important that you don't know where I take you," the man answered. "If you're ever caught, you can't tell what you don't know. Oh…and I apologize for hitting you back there."

Thomas obeyed and spent the rest of the afternoon riding around with his head in the bag. At one point he fell asleep and didn't wake up until the van came to a stop. Suddenly the door on Thomas's side of the van opened, and a gentle hand touched him. Thomas heard a voice ask in a low tone, "What's he go by?"

"Thomas Westcott," the driver answered.

"Sit up, Thomas," the new voice said softly. "I want you to leave the hood on for now and come with me."

The young refugee was helped from the van and led along a gravelly path as the sound of the van leaving could be heard behind him. After one turn and a little more walking, squeaky hinges announced the opening of a door. "We're going to walk down these steps. Duck your head a little. It's a low door."

Thomas was awkwardly assisted down a short flight of stone or concrete stairs. He was left alone for a moment, during which time he heard behind and above him the squeaky door close. "We're almost there," the voice said again. In front of him Thomas heard some heavy scraping.

"Now come with me." A hand grabbed Thomas's arm and led him forward. After a few more steps he was stopped and again heard heavy scraping behind him. A light clicked on, and the voice spoke again, "Okay, Thomas, you can remove the hood."

He found himself standing in a basement apartment illuminated by a single, overhead, neon light fixture.

"What, no firing squad?"

"Sorry about the hood," a voice said behind him. "It may not seem like it, but we *are* trying to help you."

Thomas took a moment to study his surroundings. Four small windows were located around the room close to the ceiling, but they were covered with black paint. The only furnishings were a small table with two chairs, a ragged couch, and a small bookshelf. Thomas could see a narrow doorway near one end of the room that he guessed was a bathroom. Another door across from it suggested either a closet or possibly steps leading up into the house.

"The apartment is rough, but you will be safe here until we find a permanent place for you," said the man, moving around in front of him. He was shorter than Thomas and was heavy set. The man wore a cap and had a medical mask over his face. Thomas figured he was middle aged or older since there was a lot of grey in his eyebrows.

"Where am I?" Thomas asked.

"For all of our sakes, I can't tell you that," came the answer.

"And I don't suppose you can tell me who you are," Thomas returned.

"You can call me John Smith."

"Of course," Thomas sighed, rolling his eyes. "So, you've got me locked in here, right?"

"Well, yes," Smith answered. "The doors are locked, but the locks are on the inside. You can walk out anytime you choose. I would strongly counsel you not to do that though, because with the secret police after you, your only hope is to stay with those of us who are trying to help you.

"I know you must be tired and hungry," the man continued. "I'm going to run upstairs and get you a sandwich and something to drink."

He walked to the far end of the room, opened the door Thomas had seen earlier, and disappeared up some steps. In five minutes he returned with a plate of food and a glass of water.

Sitting at the table, Thomas devoured the sandwich as the man sat across from him. "What's going to happen to me?" Thomas asked as he chewed.

"That's up to you," Mr. Smith returned. "What do you want to happen to you?"

"I don't suppose getting to live with my parents again is an option, is it?"

"I'm sorry, Thomas, but even if your parents are released and you returned to them, you would all be immediately arrested. The police hope to capture you because, by threatening to do you harm, they can pressure your parents into telling them the names of every believer your parents know."

"I don't understand why my parents would risk all this, knowing that they could be caught and sent to prison," Thomas snapped, expressing his frustration.

"For the same reason the rest of us are risking our lives and the lives of our families to help you now," Mr. Smith returned. "It's because Jesus is our King, and He wants us to do this."

Chapter Five

Thomas was tired when he stretched out on the couch to sleep, but his eyes wouldn't stay closed. There was so much on his mind. He was scared both for his parents and for his own future. His mind was also racing with questions: Who were these people who were helping him? The only thing they were getting out of all this was the chance of being arrested and thrown in prison. His own best friends wouldn't risk what these people were doing for him. Were they genuine or…

A thought came to him, and he got up and made his way out of the room. He found the steps he had descended and checked the door to the outside. Sure enough, he could unlock and open the door. It was nighttime, and he found himself staring at the dark woods that grew close to the rear of the house. He stood looking into the pitch-black shadows of the forest. He contemplated leaving and trying to make his way on his own but just as quickly put the idea aside.

I'd never make it, he thought hopelessly to himself. *I don't know where to go or what to do. How does a person start a new life from scratch anyway? I wouldn't even know where to start! It would be impossible for me to ever make it without these people. I would have already been captured if it weren't for their help. I sure wouldn't do what they're doing,* Thomas concluded. *There's no way I would risk getting arrested for helping someone…especially someone like me.*

The young man closed the door quietly and locked it from the inside. Retracing his steps in the darkness, he once again lay on the old couch. For the first time, he began to think about his life and the choices and decisions he had been making. He thought of the courage and kindness of his parents, of Aunt Faye, and of these strangers who were doing all this for him now at great risk to themselves.

After several long minutes, Thomas had to admit that these people weren't dumb or foolish. They were heroes to him. *But why?* The thought nagged him. *Why were they risking so much with no hope for return?* Then he remembered conversations that he'd had with his father more than once. Although his father had said the words with great sincerity and earnestness, they had never meant anything to him…until now. The result was that Thomas suddenly realized that these people were doing what his father had always encouraged him to do: "To live for a higher purpose than for yourself," Thomas said his father's words out loud, adding his own conclusion, "and their higher purpose is Jesus."

The next morning when Mr. Smith arrived with breakfast for his guest, he found Thomas sitting at the table reading a Bible. The young man looked at his host and lifted the book. "I...uh...found it on the bookshelf," he said. "I hope you don't mind."

"Not at all," Smith chuckled behind his mask. "That's why it's there."

"I actually know a lot about the Bible," Thomas admitted. "My parents read it to me every night and were constantly telling me things from it. I just never took what they said seriously. It was just so many stories. I guess I kind of figured that there was a God, but I never really saw what He had to do with me."

"Are you looking at it differently now?" Smith asked, taking the seat across from him.

"Yeah, I am. I've never seen faith in Jesus lived out before. Oh, I mean I have, but not like this. I expected my parents to risk their lives for me because I'm their son, but Aunt Faye and the guys who brought me here and you...I'm nothing to you, and yet you are willingly risking everything for me. Last night I couldn't understand why."

"It's because of what Jesus has done for us," Smith returned.

"That's what my parents always said," Thomas responded. "I think I'm finally starting to get it. The Bible isn't just a collection of ancient stories. This book is God speaking to me, isn't it?"

The mask hid Mr. Smith's face, but Thomas could see his eyes smiling at him. "You see, Thomas," Smith began, "God has always wanted people to genuinely love Him. But real love is a choice. No one can force you to love them. You have to choose to love. What motivates people to love God is understanding how much God loves them. The Bible says that in the book of First John. It says, *we love God because He first loved us.*"[1]

"My life has been anything but loving to God," Thomas admitted humbly.

"All of us can say that," Mr. Smith agreed. "Our sins are wicked and offensive to God's holiness. When we chose to reject God and His will for our lives, we are actually insulting Him. We are saying, 'God, I don't value You or what You say. These other things are more important to me than You or Your will.' Because God wants people to choose to love Him, He will allow people to choose not to love Him. He will let us turn away and reject Him, but then He has to reject us and give us what we ask for. In the book of Isaiah, chapter fifty-nine, the first two verses, it says that God wants to save us, but our sins are like a wall that separate us from God, which means we have to suffer the consequences for our sins, and there is no heaven waiting for us."

"Couldn't God just, sort of, say it's okay and ignore our sins?" Thomas asked.

---

[1] I John 4:19

"God isn't like us, Thomas," Smith replied. "God is always just. It's impossible for Him *not* to be just. That means sin has to be punished.

"But as bad as God's justice is for us, that's also where God's love comes in. To keep us from having to suffer the horrible punishment for sins, God loved us enough to send His Son to take the punishment for us."[2]

"You're talking about Jesus's death on the cross, right?" Thomas asked knowingly.

"Right," Mr. Smith returned. "But it was an absolutely horrible death! His enemies hit Him with their hands and fists. They beat Him with rods before they scourged him, ripping his back to pieces. They shamed and humiliated Him, shoving a crown of thorns onto His head, then hit him on the head with a stick. All of that happened before they stripped Him and nailed him to a Roman cross, leaving Him to hang there for six hours. It was the most excruciating type of death ever invented. When I think about what it cost for God to forgive my sins, it overwhelms me! And remember, Jesus had the power to stop the torture any time He wanted to, but because of His intense desire to save us, He didn't. Now that's amazing love!"

The plan was to hide Thomas for several weeks until the search for him died down, then to establish a place for him in a new location. But because of new waves of

---

[2] Romans 5:6-9

persecution, the search dragged on longer than anticipated. While Thomas waited, he and Mr. Smith had opportunities for deep talks and Bible studies. Occasionally Smith would pass on news he had received from his contacts. None of it was ever good. There had been no word about Thomas's parents. It was like they had been sucked into an enormous black hole.

Not only did Thomas fill his days with reading from the Bible and talks with Mr. Smith, but he vigorously exercised. He did hundreds of pushups and sit-ups. He opened the back door and ran up and down the steps repeatedly. After dark, when he couldn't be seen, he found a limb on a nearby tree to do pullups.

One day after he and Mr. Smith ended a prolonged study of the book of Acts in the Bible, Thomas made an announcement. "Okay, I can't run from this anymore. I'm convinced that God is real, the Bible is His word, and I believe that Jesus Christ is God's Son Whom God raised from the dead to be the Savior of the world. I am also convinced that, in spite of being an arrogant knucklehead, God loves me enough to let His Son die for me. I want you to know that I am repenting of my sins. I've lied, cheated, and stolen. I have dishonored and disobeyed my parents. I have been selfish, self-serving, and self-absorbed. I have…"

"Okay," Smith interrupted with a smile, "I get the picture."

"So let me see," Thomas said thoughtfully, "I believe in Jesus, I have repented of my sins, I have confessed my faith in Him to you just like Romans chapter ten said I should[3], and I'm ready for Jesus to be my Lord. So what is there left for me to do but to be baptized like Saul was in Acts twenty-two?"[4]

"It sounds to me like you're ready," Smith answered excitedly.

"Is there someplace to do that around here?" Thomas asked.

"Sure. We can baptize you in the bathtub. When do you want to do it?"

"Right now," Thomas returned confidently, "just like Saul in Acts chapter twenty-two, the Philippian Jailer in Acts chapter sixteen, and the Ethiopian nobleman in Acts...uh...somewhere."

"Acts eight," Mr. Smith said.

"Yes, Acts chapter eight," Thomas continued, "also like those three thousand people in Acts chapter two on the day of Pentecost. I've made my decision. I'm ready to trust Jesus with my life. Let's do it now."

"Great! I'll be right back!" Smith rushed through the door and up the stairs into his house.

Within minutes he came rushing cheerfully back down the stairs carrying an armload of towels. He walked into the bathroom and ran water into the tub. As it was filling, he placed the towels on the floor

---

[3] Romans 10:9-10
[4] Acts 22:16

around the bottom of the tub. Looking up, he saw Thomas watching curiously. "Because of your height, you'll have to lay in the tub sideways with your knees pulled up. To get you completely under the water, we'll have to fill the tub all the way to the top. That means that, when my wife and I push you under to baptize you, water's going to spill over the edge and onto the floor."

"You've done this before," Thomas said with a smile.

"Many times," Smith laughed. "I'll need my wife's help to push you under, but if you don't mind, my kids would like to be here for your baptism as well. We've all been praying for you."

Chapter Six

"Thomas!" Mr. Smith called one day as he rushed down the steps.

"What's up?" Thomas answered from where he was doing pushups beside the couch.

"I just heard from one of my contacts," Smith shot back. "It's good news! Looks like you'll be leaving soon to start your new life."

"Really?" Thomas asked excitedly.

"Really," Smith returned with a smile. "I know you've been anxious to finally take the next step in your journey."

"Yeah, I have," the young man returned nervously. "Do you know where I'll be going?"

"The word that I received is that there is a believing couple in Grantham who have agreed to take you in and help you."

"Grantham?!" Thomas said with surprise. "Are you serious? That's a big city. Is that safe? I thought I'd be relocating out in the country somewhere."

"The easiest place to hide is in a crowd," Mr. Smith returned with a smile. "Don't worry. You aren't the first person we've relocated there, and so far it's worked out great. You'll have lots of brothers and sisters there to support you, plus we have a placement organization in Grantham to help refugees find their way."

"What will I do once I get there?" Thomas asked timidly.

"What we really need to talk about right now is the direction you're going to take from this point on."

"I don't understand," Thomas said with a confused look.

"Look, my friend," Smith began, "because of God's grace, you are getting an amazing opportunity. You are starting a completely new life…in more ways than one. The choices and decisions you make for this new life of yours are going to be very important ones."

"What do you mean?" Thomas asked.

"Thomas, are you going to do like most people and try to keep a low profile and just get by, hoping not to be noticed by the police? Or are you grateful to God and ready to use the rest of your life to do things that have eternal significance?"

Thomas sat back on the couch thoughtfully. "Wow! What a question! I guess I thought I would just hide out someplace and sort of, you know, disappear."

"Don't get me wrong, you will definitely be living in the shadows, so to speak, as long as the police are looking for you," Smith answered. "But that's not what I'm talking about. What's going to be your direction from this moment on? Are you going to be focused on yourself, or are you going to live for a higher purpose? Why do you think God saved you?"

"I've wondered that many times," Thomas returned, "and to be honest, I really don't know."

"Well, maybe a better question to ask is, 'Who did God put you on this earth to be?'"

"I would love to know the answer to that question," Thomas returned. "How do you know who God wants you to be?"

"Have you asked Him?"

"No, I haven't. Does God answer questions like that? Does He actually speak to you?"

"Why wouldn't He?" Smith responded sincerely. "After all, He is your Father, and you are His son. Satan talks to you, doesn't he?"

"Oh, wow, yeah…all the time!"

"Well," Smith returned, "if Satan, who hates you, talks to you, doesn't it make sense that your loving Father in Heaven talks to you as well? Jesus did say, *My sheep hear My voice.*[5] You are one of His sheep, right?"

"Yeah," Thomas answered confidently, "I absolutely am one of His sheep."

"Okay, so, if you're His sheep, He speaks to you, and you hear His voice. Ask Him who He has called

---

[5] John 10:27

you to be. Then tell me what He says, because I'm really interested."

Later that evening as Thomas was alone in the apartment, he got down on his knees beside the old couch and asked God the question that he desperately wanted the answer to: "Holy Father in Heaven, I know You love me, and You have worked hard to bring me to the place where I trust in You and in Your Son, my Lord Jesus Christ. I have even learned to trust You in the things that I don't understand.

"Up until recently I lived totally for myself. I believed the lie that I was here to get all the pleasure and enjoyment that I could out of this life. I don't believe that anymore. I have been put on this earth to live for You...But, Father, I don't know what that looks like. Lord, please tell me who You've called me to be."

As he sat there in silent anticipation, the words *holy ninja* popped in his mind. He immediately rebuked himself for letting his own foolish thoughts highjack his prayer, and he tried again. After repeated attempts, that first phrase was the only response he received. Frustrated, he rolled onto the couch and went to sleep.

The next day as he was getting ready to leave, Mr. Smith asked him if God had spoken to him.

"Well...uh...I don't really think so," Thomas answered with a look of embarrassment.

Smith gave him a questioning look.

"Okay, I did ask God who He created me to be, and I did get an answer, but I don't think it was from God."

"What did you hear?"

"Um…holy ninja."

"Hmm," Smith returned thoughtfully. "That's different."

"Yeah, I know," Thomas answered sheepishly. "I think my mind was just wandering. It does that a lot. I'll try asking again, but I think before I do that, I will read some scripture. Maybe that will help me stay focused."

"Keep asking Him, Thomas," Smith said. "God has a specific plan for what He wants you to do with your life."

"Do you think so?" the young man asked.

"Oh, I'm sure of it," Mr. Smith answered with a look of confidence. "Think back on all that God has done to save you and bring you to faith in Him. By all rights, you should have been arrested with your parents."

"I like to think that God has a plan for me," Thomas returned. "I'm not sure what it might be right now, but I know what my parents would want me to do. After all that Jesus has done for me, I now agree with what they used to say. I want to be like my parents and do things that have eternal significance. But, Mr. Smith, I'm going to be honest with you, that sounds really scary."

"You could look at it like that," Smith returned, "or you could see it as the adventure of a lifetime." He paused. "You know what, Thomas? God might just need a holy ninja to accomplish it!"

Chapter Seven

Twelve weeks later Thomas stood on a street corner on the east side of the metropolis of Grantham drinking a cup of green tea. He cast nervous glances around but saw nothing suspicious. As he took another sip of his drink, he looked at the side of the cup to recheck the note written there. *Thornton and Reedy 10:15.*

Thomas looked at the street signs to be sure he was at the right location. He then stole a glance at his cheap digital watch and saw 10:12. *Right place, right time,* he reassured himself as he watched with interest the cars that occasionally passed. Three minutes later a sixteen-passenger van with the name *J. J. Transportation* on the front door pulled to a stop beside him, and the side door slid open.

"I'm shocked! You actually made it this time, and fully dressed too!" a man's voice called teasingly from the van.

"Give me a break, Mike," Thomas shot back as he stepped into the van. "Last week wasn't my fault. I had…uh…an intense emergency. Seriously, it took all my skills to deal with it!"

"So glad to see that you didn't have to unclog another toilet today," Mike said loudly enough for the other twelve passengers to hear.

The others in the van responded with smiles and a few soft chuckles at Thomas's red face and sheepish grin.

Mike Schuster was a good friend to Thomas. When the young refugee had first been brought to the large city of Grantham, it was Mike and his wife, Penny, who had agreed to take Thomas in to help him get started with his new secret life as a believer in Jesus. The young exile had been sent to live with the Schuster's in their two-bedroom flat located just above the Cup O' Joy coffee shop Mike owned and operated on the lower east side of the city. Mike and his wife had treated Thomas like family from the first, and it had been a great blessing for the young believer. Eventually they found an apartment for Thomas near them, and the apartment manager had agreed to hire Thomas as handyman in exchange for his rent. It all worked out really well.

Mike had also connected Thomas with a butcher, and the young fugitive earned money for food and other expenses by working part-time making deliveries. In addition Thomas did the occasional odd job for Mike as well as some of the other people in the neighborhood.

As soon as the van pulled away from the curb, all the riders started a discrete worship time of songs, shared scriptures, and prayers. This was the Schuster's house church, although today it was a van church.

Mike and the other leaders tried to vary the meeting days, times, and locations to protect the members from discovery as much as possible.

After their time of worship, Mike asked anyone who wished to share how God had revealed Himself to them this week, and five of them told their stories. Another one of the men quoted a scripture that he had been studying, and the group spent several minutes discussing what it meant to them. With the constant threat of persecution, these times together were precious to the believers, and everyone felt a responsibility to bring something to encourage the others. After the sharing time, and as the van cruised slowly around the city park, Mike reported what news he had received from the other groups of believers in town. There was quite a long period of discussion on the needs and problems of several of the house churches in the city. Mike reported that the west side of town was experiencing heavier attacks than usual.

"It's because there is a new Deputy Administrator for the city," one of the men in the back of the van offered. "His name is Devlin Trask, and he's trying to make a name for himself in the ruling party by cracking down on Christians. All of us need to expect the attacks to spill over onto our side of town real soon. Get ready, everybody, because it's coming!"

"That means that we need to be extra careful," Mike admonished them, "and remember to be in constant prayer for our brothers and sisters across town."

"There has to be more that we can do to help them!" one of the ladies stated with feeling. "Wives and husbands have lost their mates, children have lost their parents, and parents have lost their children."

Tears formed in the corner of Thomas's eyes as he listened, and his thoughts turned to his own parents, as they often did.

"Actually, there may be something that can be done to help them," Mike announced. "Some of us have been discussing that very thing."

"Can you tell us about it?" someone asked.

"You know how it is, Nate," Mike answered evasively. "The less you know, the better. I would encourage all of you be asking God to show us His plans."

"Do you really think something could be done to genuinely help those folks?" Nate asked.

"I can't say much," Mike returned, "but the people involved are asking for God-sized things, if you know what I mean."

Mike gave a signal to the driver, and as they spent a prolonged time in group prayer, the van pulled to the curb at each predetermined stop, allowing the believers to disembark where they were picked up.

As Mike and his wife took their turn to leave, he spoke to Thomas. "Come with us. I want you to meet someone…plus, we'll feed you lunch."

Thomas's eyebrows went up. "Food?" he asked with a gleam in his eyes and followed them out of the van.

Thomas and Mike waited outside the closed coffee shop as Mike's wife hurried upstairs to grab their meal.

"We aren't going up?" Thomas asked curiously.

"Not today," Mike answered. "We're having a picnic. You like picnics, don't you?"

"No offense, Mike, but the answer is, I like food, especially your wife's food, and I don't really care where it's at."

Mike just laughed and shook his head. "Okay, okay, we'll feed you! But you're going to have to wait until we get to the park."

When his wife returned, Mike took the basket from her, and they walked down the block to the city park. He led them to the small lake in the middle of the grassy common and spread a blanket beside a bench where a man wearing a hat and sunglasses sat fishing.

As Mike's wife removed the hand-made meal from the basket and spread it on the blanket, Thomas heard a voice say, "Is this the guy?" It was uttered by the fisherman, who didn't bother to turn in their direction.

"Yes," Mike answered while he reached for a sandwich.

"Has he got a handle?" the fisherman spoke again, adjusting his line.

Mike looked at Thomas and asked, "What's your favorite number?"

A little confused, Thomas thought for a moment and answered, "Forty-five."

"You can call him *Forty-five*," Mike said, addressing the fisherman but not looking at him.

For the next thirty minutes the strange man asked Thomas a number of questions about himself. Thomas took his cue from Mike and never looked at the man when he answered.

There was silence for several minutes after the man took in all of the information Thomas had given him. Finally he said to Mike, "Coffee Man, you know what's at stake here. Do you trust him?"

"Completely," Mike answered smiling at Thomas.

Just then the fisherman reeled in his line, grabbed his tackle box, and stood up. When he walked past the picnickers, a folded piece of paper dropped into Thomas's lap.

The young believer ignored the paper for a few minutes as the fisherman walked away. Finally he reached down and stealthily picked up the note. "I don't understand," Thomas said without looking at the message. "What is this?"

"It's the opportunity all of us have been praying for," Mike answered. "Thomas, it's a chance to finally do something to help those poor folks who are suffering for Christ."

Chapter Eight

The message had said to go that evening. The address was for a building Thomas was not familiar with, so he spent over an hour studying the city map until he was confident he knew how to get there. The note had also stated that, when he traveled to the meeting, it was critically important that he not be followed. So an hour and a half before he was to arrive, Thomas climbed the stairs to the roof of his apartment building wearing dark pants, a dark hoodie, and a dark neck warmer that he could pull up over his face should it be needed.

It was nighttime, but the moon was up, and he could see well enough. Hurrying over to the north edge of the building, Thomas took a moment to view the narrow alley below. He carefully studied the distance between his building and the next one. *Just like back home with Beans and Garrett*, he thought with a nostalgic smile.

Trotting back ten steps, Thomas confidently raced to the ledge and leaped.

An hour and twenty minutes later, he was standing on the roof of the building where his meeting was to be held. He studied the surrounding buildings as well as the streets below. Detecting nothing unusual, he trotted to the rear of the building and slipped over the ledge. The protruding edges of the corner blocks of the structure gave Thomas the grips and the toe holds that he needed to swiftly descend the eight stories. Once on the ground, he kept to the shadows as he strolled cautiously around to the front. Beside the door was a panel containing a long list of apartment numbers, each with a button beside it. Thomas pressed the one by the number that he had memorized from the note.

"Yes?" a female voice spoke through the speaker.

"Forty-Five," the young man announced. A moment later the electric lock on the door buzzed open, and he entered.

Thomas had never liked elevators; they were too confining. Racing up the dark stairway, he passed as lightly and as quietly as a cat. He wasn't even breathing hard when he reached the fifth floor. Studying the apartment doors, he soon found the one numbered five twenty-eight. The note had said, "Don't knock. Walk in. Close door." The knob turned, and he cautiously stepped inside the dark room, obediently shutting the door behind him.

"Lock it and don't turn on the light," a soft voice came from the shadows across the room.

Thomas obeyed.

"There is a chair three steps in front of you," the voice said. "Make yourself comfortable."

Thomas found the chair in the dark and sat down.

"Thank you for coming, Forty-five. We know you have lots of questions, but first we need to find out more about you. To begin with, tell us about your relationship with Jesus."

For almost an hour Thomas sat in the darkness and reviewed his spiritual journey of both running from God and being drawn to Him. The mysterious speaker seemed to already know most of the facts Thomas related about himself but was most interested in his thoughts and attitudes toward Jesus. He wasn't sure where all of this was leading, but Thomas felt strongly that he must be honest with his questioners. He admitted his original anger and bitterness towards his parents, but also how that had all changed when he met Jesus.

There were some questions about his physical skills, but it seemed to be his genuine admiration for his parents' commitment to serving Christ, even though it had resulted in their arrest, that convinced the speaker.

"How would you describe yourself?" the interviewer asked.

Thomas thought about that for a moment. How would he describe himself? So much had changed in him within the last few months. Jesus had done so much in him that he seemed to himself to be a totally different person. The things that used to be so important to him weren't important at all anymore.

"Hmm…Well, I'd have to say that I'm a follower of Jesus who wants to use my life and all my abilities to serve God and bring Him glory…and I would also really like to save my parents."

There was a long period of silence after that. Eventually the voice spoke again. "You can turn on the light now."

Thomas felt his way back to the front door and flipped the switch beside it. Thomas was surprised. There was no one else in the room.

"I'm sorry Forty-five, but we had to be careful," the voice spoke. Thomas's eyes searched the room and discovered a small speaker and microphone on a coffee table in front of the chair he had been sitting in. "We've decided that we want to talk with you about our plans. Continue to apartment eight zero five. We are waiting for you there."

When Thomas arrived at the correct door, he was unsure as to whether he should walk in as he did before or knock. Finally, he knocked tentatively. After a moment he heard the door being unlocked, and it cracked open. The eyes looking out studied him for a moment, then the door swung open, and he was beckoned inside.

Thomas was surprised at who awaited him. A nicely dressed, middle-aged woman held the door.

"Please sit down, Forty-five," said a young man close to Thomas's age who was sitting in a wheelchair behind a desk covered with computer screens and electronic equipment. "We have been praying for someone like you for a long time."

Thomas took the offered chair near the man at the desk. The woman sat in a second chair close to both of them. "We have been peppering you with questions for an hour," the woman said as she stared deeply into Thomas's eyes. "It's only fair that we let you ask yours now."

Thomas opened his mouth but was cut off by the man in the wheelchair. "Wait a minute!" He spun around and typed quickly on his keyboard. Suddenly classical music began to fill the room. "No one should be listening to us," he announced rapidly as he turned back to the others, "but I like to be cautious."

"Okay," Thomas began, "you know a lot about me, so who are you?"

"You can call me Egg," the wheelchair bound man answered, spewing out words as fast as his fingers had raced across his keyboard, "and you can call my friend here O.G.P." Thomas noticed a slight smile briefly crossing the woman's face at Egg's words.

"I'm assuming that all of this has something to do with trying to help some of the believers across town who are in trouble right now?" Thomas questioned.

"Yes," Egg shot back, "but we hope to reach much further than just across town. Reports come to us daily of followers of Jesus who have great needs because of the persecution. O.G.P., several others, and myself have been planning and preparing ways to help them for over a year."

"But what can be done?" Thomas asked.

"Hopefully, quite a bit," O.G.P. returned. "We have spent a year establishing connections within some of the government agencies as well as inside the secret police. We even have underground Christian contacts deep within the government's New Self Church."

"We have the resources," Egg announced proudly as he patted the powerful computers next to him. "O.G.P. and a couple of other wealthy followers of Christ have offered their fortunes for this work."

Thomas turned to look at the woman with her serious, business-like air. "My family was very successful in manufacturing before we lost our freedoms," O.G.P. said. "The new government thought they had confiscated my father's fortune, but he actually was able to hide a substantial amount from them."

"Our plans are finally ready," Egg said, taking up the discourse again. "All we needed were a few trusted operatives. You should round out our team very nicely…if you are willing to join us."

"You need to understand that you will face great risk to be a part of this work," O.G.P. emphasized.

At this point both Egg and the woman stared expectantly at him, and Thomas realized that they were waiting for his answer. He stood and began pacing the room. Thomas found it difficult to pray on his knees as his hyperactive mind tended to wander when he was still. Somehow moving helped him to concentrate. *Holy Father in Heaven,* he prayed in his heart, *this is what I have always been afraid of. The risk of offending the government authorities terrifies me, and it's what I've spent most of my life running and hiding from. Through my parents and people like these, You are showing me the cost of following Jesus Christ…and Father, I have at last come to believe that He is worth it! I'll admit that I'm scared, Lord, but this is my chance to do something to maybe help my parents and many others of Your followers who are suffering simply because they love Jesus. Father, I need Your help more than I ever have in my life because I'm really afraid, but I believe You've called me to do things of eternal significance, and this is one of those things! Holy Father, I reject the fear, and I will be Your holy ninja!*

Chapter Nine

After several minutes of talking with O.G.P., it was clear to Thomas that she was a very smart woman. Saying that Egg was smart just didn't seem accurate. He was stunningly brilliant!

"So, who are we?" Thomas asked, wondering what he had just become a part of.

"We are God's invisible hands and feet for those who suffer in His name," O.G.P. said confidently.

"For those overwhelmed by the darkness," Egg added, "we are the lamps of the Lord. But due to the nature of our secret work, the Lord has allowed our lamps to remain hidden under the proverbial bushel."

"Invisible hands and feet...hidden lamps," Thomas said his thoughts out loud. "I'm still confused. As those who will work in the shadows, how will we accomplish these very visible tasks?"

"I've been in this wheelchair all my life," Egg explained. "Since God has kept me from doing much with my body, I decided He wanted me to use my brain. So I use it for Him."

"Egg has come up with some innovative ideas to deal with the problems that we face," O.G.P. added. "Explain to him your communications network, Egg."

"I was wondering how we are to get messages to each other without the government listening in," Thomas said. "I know that cell phones are out of the question because the government constantly monitors all the calls. Do you use radios with some special frequency?"

"No," Egg answered casually. "We don't transmit with radio waves; we use lasers."

"How is that possible?" Thomas asked in shock.

"A transmitted radio signal can pass through a laser just like it can through a wire," Egg explained, "but no one can listen in unless they intercept the beam of light through which the transmission is taking place. Therefore, we place the lasers in hard to get to locations so that unwanted interception is very difficult. Admittedly, using lasers does limit us a bit, but our communications are secure."

And that's how Thomas found himself a few hours later on top of his apartment building with a backpack full of Egg's electronic equipment. In the center of the roof was a four-foot square and three-foot high slotted metal box used for the apartment building's ventilation. Attached to the side of it was a rectangular tower made of small steel girders, on top of which was attached the antennae for receiving government television programming. The tower was over twenty feet tall and seemed solid to Thomas when he gripped it.

Using a pair of night vision goggles also supplied by Egg, Thomas spread out his equipment and checked his notes. Repacking his backpack and slinging it on his shoulders, he cautiously scaled the tower. When he reached the top, Thomas noticed that the night breeze made the tower sway slightly, giving him a nervous feeling in his stomach. *I guess this probably isn't a good time to be wondering how long this tower has been here and if the bolts holding it are screwed in nice and tight,* Thomas nervously thought to himself. Ignoring the fear, he slid off the pack and clipped it to one of the girders so that everything he needed was close at hand.

He pulled out the plastic tube with Egg's laser firmly attached inside. Using a small compass, he mounted the laser tube securely to the tower with the special brackets Egg had built for it, making sure it was pointed in the right direction. Beside it he hung a rechargeable battery, and attached to it, he mounted a small solar panel to provide electricity to keep the battery charged.

When those tasks were completed, Thomas pulled a small box out of his pack and turned it on. Typing in the code Egg had given him, he clipped it to the laser tube. Thomas saw a set of coordinates appear on the screen. *Okay,* Thomas said to himself, *those are the exact coordinates from here to the relay tower a mile away.* Thomas slowly turned the small knobs on the bottom and side of the bracket holding the tube containing the laser. The device began to move in tiny increments. Once the alignment matched the coordinates on the screen, he flipped on the laser and spoke into the microphone. "Test broadcast from Forty-five. Test broadcast from Forty-five."

There was only a brief pause, then a faint voice spoke in his earpiece, "I read you, Forty-five, but you are weak."

"Give me a count," Thomas returned, and the voice in his earpiece began to count up from one. As Thomas listened, he slowly adjusted the small knobs as Egg had instructed until he could hear the voice clearly. "I've got it!" Thomas finally announced.

He was just getting ready to turn off the laser and go to bed when the voice in his earpiece spoke again, "We have a project for you, Forty-five."

"What is it?" Thomas listened with interest as Egg explained the role he was to play.

"When?" Thomas asked.

"One up sixteen," came the secretive answer.

One up sixteen? Thomas mumbled to himself as he climbed down the tower, carefully zip-tying the wire from the laser to the girders as he descended. Once he was standing on the roof, he used a rechargeable screwdriver to attach the small metal device into which the wire disappeared to the side of the ventilation box with long sheet metal screws. Grabbing his pack, Thomas quickly descended the stairs and hurried to his apartment.

One up sixteen, he repeated to himself. *What did Egg tell me about that? The first number is the day. So 'one' is Sunday; that's today. Then 'up sixteen.' Egg said he uses Jewish time. The Jewish day starts at six p.m. So 'up sixteen' means I add sixteen hours to six pm. That's ten a.m. Monday morning.*

Thomas quickly checked his city map and found where he was to be at ten the next morning. *Oh wow!* Thomas thought to himself. *That's the Security Administration Building…talk about walking into the lion's den. I should get there a little early to scope out a good escape route if I need one. I'll have some explaining to do to my boss when I get back later than normal to start work,* he thought to himself, *but I'd better leave here by eight thirty.* He then immediately got ready for bed.

Nine fifty-five Monday morning found Thomas in his dark hoodie standing near the front entrance of the Security Administration Office Building. He loitered on the sidewalk, pretending to read his map. At two minutes past ten, he noticed several people walk out of the building. One was a young woman in a knee-length navy skirt, a white blouse, and a red scarf. Thomas watched her cross the street and enter a small park.

Still pretending to study his map, he followed her at a distance. He watched her walk up to a coffee kiosk and order a large, hot drink. After receiving it, she sat on a nearby park bench.

Thomas also ordered a large drink. Paying for it, he took his cup and approached the woman, who had set her drink beside her on the bench. Seating himself and setting his own cup in front of hers, Thomas opened his map and said, "Excuse me, but do you know how to get to…"

"DO I LOOK LIKE A TOUR GUIDE?" the girl snapped and stood up quickly, grabbing Thomas's cup.

"I was just asking…" Thomas sputtered, shocked at the girl's reaction.

"WELL, ASK SOMEONE ELSE, CREEP!"

As the girl stormed back to the office building, a man in a suit standing nearby came up to her. "Is that guy bothering you, Grace?" he asked as he stared hard at the hooded figure on the bench.

"Just some loser looking for a date," she snapped. "Thanks, Kyle."

As the suited man escorted the young woman back into the building, Thomas picked up the drink that was left. Slipping his hand stealthily beneath the cup, he felt the flash drive he had come for stuck to the bottom.

Thomas took one last look at the woman and noticed that the man in the suit made a subtle move with one of his hands. Cutting his eyes around, Thomas noticed another suited figure standing nearby fold his newspaper and begin moving toward him. With no more hesitation, Thomas stood up and walked purposefully out of the park, across the street, and toward the end of a nearby building. As he disappeared around the corner, Thomas glanced back and saw the man hurrying to catch up to him.

As soon as the suited police agent lost sight of the hooded figure he was tailing, he rushed to the edge of the building around which Thomas had darted. Whipping into the alley, the policeman saw that it was empty except for a cup of coffee tossed hastily on the ground thirty feet ahead of him.

"He's running!" the agent exclaimed out loud and raced down the alley to catch his prey.

Thomas watched all of this as he hung from a windowsill two floors above the alley. As soon as his pursuer was gone, Thomas dropped quietly to the pavement. Checking to be sure no one was watching, he pulled off his hoodie, rolled it up, and stuck it under his arm. Then he smugly patted the flash drive in his pocket as he casually strolled back to his apartment.

Chapter Ten

"So what's on this thing?" Thomas asked as he rolled the flash drive between his fingers.

"We won't be sure till we look," Egg answered as he took the drive from Thomas and quickly shoved it into a port on his computer, "but it's supposed to be the list of prisoners the government has taken."

"Will it have my parents on there?" Thomas asked eagerly.

"It should if our people were able to get the lists."

"We hope it will also contain where each prisoner is being held," added O.G.P., who was also present. "If we can make that information public and generate enough noise about it, maybe the government will be less likely to torture them."

"Do you think we might be able to get them out?" Thomas asked again.

"We'll have to see," returned O.G.P. "We have to take one step at a time and see what doors God opens for us."

Egg's fingers flew over the keys as he opened the files on the flash drive. "The list is here," he finally announced, "but I can't find the names of any of our people on it!"

"None of them?" O.G.P. asked with concern.

"Nope…none!"

"Maybe it's an old list," Thomas suggested.

"I don't think so," Egg shot back. "G.C. knew what we needed."

"G.C.?" Thomas asked.

"The female operative who gave you the drive."

"Oh, Grace!"

Both Egg and O.G.P. turned and looked at Thomas when he mentioned her name.

"I…uh…heard one of the police agents call her name when she was walking back into the building."

Turning back to his computer, Egg said his thoughts out loud. "Maybe this other file has more names." After double clicking on the file icon and studying the contents for a few minutes, Egg shook his head. "It's just a long string of code. I can't tell what it is. I think it might be some kind of a command sequence."

"We need to contact G.C.," Egg's well-dressed companion announced. "She should be available now. See if you can reach her."

Egg quickly wheeled his chair to his communications console, clicked a dial two notches, and pushed a button on the panel. Within a minute a voice crackled over the speaker. Egg turned down the volume so that the noise wouldn't carry out of the room.

"Did you get it?" the female voice asked.

"I'm looking at the contents now," Egg answered, "but we can't find any of our people."

There was a moment's pause, then the voice crackled back from the speaker. "That's because we found out that anytime someone is arrested, the detention authorities assign them new names before they are put in the computer system. That way the government can make their prisoners disappear. At least, that's what Juice was told."

"Juice?" Thomas asked.

"Another of our operatives in the government's administrative division. Juice is one of their main data entry people. He's the reason we were able to get this flash drive. G.C. was just the courier to get it to you."

"If they've changed the prisoners' names, there's no way we can figure out where our people are!" O.G.P. said angrily.

"We'll figure it out," Egg said confidently. "We'll just need to work harder.

"G.C.," Egg said into the microphone, "there's another file here that's nothing but code. What's that about?"

"Well, since we couldn't give you the actual names you wanted," the voice in the speaker said, "Juice thought we should give you the next best thing. Egg, Juice says that you are to look in the dark space. Oh, and if that guy in the hoodie is there, tell him I'm sorry for yelling at him. Got to go."

"Hey, she apologized!" Thomas said with a smile. "That's cool! You know, she was actually really cute…in sort of…an in-your-face kind of way. So, who is she, Egg? Maybe she likes me!"

Suddenly an elbow shot into Thomas's side.

"What?" Thomas asked, looking at O.G.P. as he rubbed his sore ribs.

"Just because she apologized to you doesn't mean she wants to marry you!"

"You never know," Thomas returned with a dreamy look. "You weren't there. While she was yelling at me, she had this…*look*…in her eye."

"Oh, good grief!"

"I'm serious. It's something us guys pick up on. Isn't that right, Egg?"

But Egg wasn't listening. He was mumbling *look in the dark space* to himself.

"What does *look in the dark space* mean?" O.G.P. asked as she looked at the computer screen over Egg's shoulder.

"Juice has hidden a note or some special instructions on the flash drive," Egg answered.

"So the message is hidden somewhere in the dark space of the drive?" Thomas asked with a confused look.

"In a way…but not really," Egg said as he worked feverishly on the keyboard. "*In the dark space* just means there's a hidden file on the drive."

"You can do that?"

"Sure," Egg returned, still typing. "You just need to know to look for them, which we now know. And then you need to know how to find them, which I do. And….there it is!"

"What does it say?" O.G.P. asked, leaning closer.

"OH, WOW!" Egg exclaimed as he sat back in his wheelchair, bumping into O.G.P.

"What is it?" Thomas asked. "It doesn't per chance have Grace's phone number, does it?"

"Would you stop?!"

"This is awesome!" Egg exclaimed, ignoring his companions. "Juice has apparently been secretly creating a backdoor into the government's secure server for several months…and it's finally ready!"

"Did you know Juice was working on this?" O.G.P. asked.

"No," Egg said with a laugh. "It was something he was doing on the sly. The people in charge of the government's computers just think Juice is a data entry typist. They obviously have no clue how tech savvy and smart he is, or they never would have let him close to their stuff.

"There's a web address in this message," Egg continued, "that allows my computer to reach Juice's backdoor. Then by using that string of code in the file, we can open it."

"Then what?" Thomas asked.

"Then I should be able to spend all the time I want searching through every file they've got. Don't worry, O.G.P. We'll find our people."

"That's great!" Thomas said encouragingly. "But I figure that's going to take some time. Is there anything you want me to do?"

"Two things actually," Egg said as he wheeled over to a chest and lifted the lid. "Here, put this in your backpack." Egg handed him a small device that looked like a cross between a pistol and a mini satellite dish.

"*Heh, heh…*What's this…a ray gun?"

"You read too many comic books," an annoyed Egg shot back. "It's an electronic listening device. There are ear buds located in the bottom of the handle that go with it. Turn it on and point it at people you need to listen to, and you can hear their conversation from over two hundred yards away.

"Seriously?" Thomas asked in amazement as he stared at the device.

"Yes, seriously," Egg returned.

"That's awesome!" Thomas exclaimed with a big grin. "Uh…What do you want me to do with it?"

"I want you to practice using it, so when you need it, you know how to operate it. There are times that you will need to listen in on conversations at a distance.

Here's the power adapter. Be sure and always keep it charged up."

"You said there were two things you wanted me to do."

Egg turned and looked at O.G.P.

"Forty-five, are you a member of the government's New Self Church?" O.G.P. asked.

"No, of course not," Thomas shot back as he shoved the listening device into his pack. "Why would I do that?"

"Because we have operatives in various levels of the church, and if you were a regular attender, we could use you to get information from them to us."

"You mean right there in the government's own church? That's crazy!"

"The next church meeting is tomorrow night at six thirty. It's the church campus on Poplar Street. Be there…get involved…and no flirting with the girls!"

"Oh, I would never do that!" Thomas answered with a mischievous look. "Grace wouldn't like it."

Chapter Eleven

Shortly after nine o'clock the next night, Thomas was walking back to his apartment from the large New Self Church building. He was impressed at how polished the presentation was. *I should have expected that,* he thought to himself. *Everything the government does to promote itself is going to be top notch. But I am surprised at how many people they have conned into working for them. Surely all those people in the classy shirts aren't paid staff! They were all over the place! And if I have to talk to another over-the-top enthusiastic person with a fake smile on their face, I'm going to hit someone! Maybe now that I've joined up, they'll stop pestering me.*

When he arrived back at his apartment, he couldn't relax. He was so tense from listening to propaganda for the last two hours that he needed to do something to unwind. He glanced over at his backpack and smiled. Snatching it up, he hurried to the roof.

He found a spot at the southwest corner of the building where he could see several other apartment buildings. Reaching into his pack, he pulled out Egg's listening device. After studying it for several minutes with his flashlight, he pulled the ear buds from their compartment in the handle, stuck them in his ears, and turned on the device. He winced as a loud squeal sounded directly in his ears. Quickly turning the volume down, he began to play with the settings.

Leaning over the low wall of the roof, he pointed the receiving disc at the street below. He didn't hear much at first except the roar of an occasional passing vehicle. Suddenly he was startled by a cough that was as loud as if the person was sitting beside him. Looking down, he saw the listening device was pointed at a man standing beneath a light pole two blocks away. "Whoa!" Thomas gasped out loud.

He saw the door of a bar a block away swing open, and a man paused in the opening to say his goodbyes. Quickly Thomas aimed the powerful microphone at him. "Okay, I'll talk to the guys, Ned. But I'm tellin' ya', if you want to join our bowling team, you gotta get your scores up." There was a pause as he listened to his friend who was still inside the building respond. Then the man said, "Yeah, yeah, yeah…whatever.

"What a goob!" the man said under his breath as he left the bar. "That guy bowls like a drunk monkey."

Wow! Thomas thought to himself. *This thing is so sensitive!* He studied the area below him, looking for another victim, but none showed up. Just then he spotted a dark SUV turn onto the street and approach his building.

"I'll bet that's a cop," Thomas said out loud as he watched the car draw near. He saw that the window was down, so he pointed his device at the passing car.

"Turning left on Phillips Street," the driver said, and Thomas could hear the clear clicking of the man's turn signal.

"Roger that," responded a crackly voice from the radio in the car.

Thomas heard more instructions coming over the policeman's radio, but the car turned and was lost to his view.

For the next five minutes, Thomas could find no one else to practice on. He knew he should probably go to bed, but he wasn't tired of playing with his new toy. On a whim he began pointing it at some of the windows in the apartment building across the street, just to see if he could detect anything through the glass. From most of the windows, all he got was silence, although he did hear music from one and snoring from another.

He was about to call it a night and go to bed when he heard a pleading voice from one of the windows about a half-block away, "Please, Mom, don't drink anymore!"

"Leave me alone and go to bed, Josh!" a woman's voice shot back angrily. "You don' un'erstand what I go through ever'day!"

"But I'm hungry!" the boy whined.

"Did you finish the crackers?"

"Yes."

"Well, I don' have anything else," his mother returned. "Just drink some water and go to bed. I'll try to come up with somethin' tomorrow."

Thomas kept the listening device pointed at the window and heard footsteps and a door shut. There was a brief pause, then soft crying sounded in his ear buds.

When he heard the door close, Thomas noticed a light turn on in the window beside the one at which his device was pointed. Directing the powerful microphone at this new opening, he heard a sad boy's voice praying loudly enough for his mother to hear in the next room. "Dear Jesus, I know I'm not supposed to be talking to You, but we're in trouble! Please help Mom and me! We've got nothing to eat, and I'm really hungry. Could You give us some food? Peanut butter and jelly and bread would be okay. And please help my Mom, Lord! She can't find a job, and she gets worried. That's when she starts drinking. It's getting really bad, Jesus! Can You please help us? Oh…and if You bring us some jelly, can You please make it grape? Amen."

Thomas was wiping away tears as he put his listening device back into his pack. He hurried down to his apartment and went through his jar of money.

"Hmm…Thirty bucks. I can't get much with that," he said out loud, "but I can make a start."

Thomas stuffed the cash in his pocket, scribbled out a note, and raced out the door. He ran to the Quickie Mart four blocks away and grabbed bread, peanut butter, milk, and a squirt bottle of grape jelly. He put all his purchases and his note in a small cardboard box he found and raced back to the apartment building where Josh and his mother lived.

When he was sure he had located Josh's bedroom window, Thomas hurried to the end of the building and put his box on the ground. Jumping up to grab the fire escape ladder, he pulled it down and snatched up the box, rushing up the steps until he reached the third floor. The ledge was wide enough to stand on, so he began carefully working his way along until he had reached Josh's window. Thomas balanced the carton on the ledge, making sure that it would not fall off, then he knocked several times loudly on the window.

When the light in the room came on, Thomas retreated back the way he had come. He could hear the boy shout when he saw the box outside his window. "MOM! MOM! COME HERE QUICK! THERE'S A BOX OF STUFF ON THE LEDGE! QUICK, MOM, QUICK!"

Thomas froze in the shadows as he heard the window slide open.

"LOOK, MOM, LOOK! IT'S EVERYTHING I PRAYED FOR!"

"This is crazy! How did a box of food get on the third-floor ledge?! What does that note say?"

"It says, 'Dear Josh, I heard your prayer. This is just the first installment. I love you, Jesus. P.S. Keep praying. I love it!' MOM, IT'S FROM JESUS! HE HEARD MY PRAYER!

"What does *installment* mean?"

"It means," his mother answered, "that more is coming." Thomas could tell she was crying when she spoke.

Hee, hee, hee, Thomas chuckled to himself. *Thank You for letting me do that, Lord. Sometimes this holy ninja stuff is really fun! Now please show me where the rest of the money is going to come from so I can deliver the motherlode for You.*

Chapter Twelve

Thomas was up bright and early the next morning. He knew Mike opened the Cup o' Joy at seven for business people getting their coffee before work. As he pushed through the front door, he saw a woman at the front just paying Maddie, Mike's employee, for her coffee. Rushing eagerly up beside her, Thomas called impatiently to his friend. "Mike, Mike!"

"Well, you're here awfully early," Mike Schuster called from the drink prep area.

"I need you to help me with a special project!" Thomas said with a big grin.

"Oh, hey! It's you!" This was said by the young woman who just purchased the coffee.

Thomas gave a start when he saw the woman. It was G.C.! "Wow!" Thomas returned excitedly. "Imagine running into you here!"

"So what's your project?" Mike asked, pulling his friend back on topic.

"Okay, so I've found this needy family, and I want to buy them some groceries. I used most of my cash getting them some stuff, but it wasn't enough food. I wanted to see if you would let me mop out your shop tonight for some extra money."

Mike cut his eyes to the girl working behind the counter.

"It's okay with me," Maddie said with a grin. "I'd love to get off early."

"We close at six this evening," Mike said to Thomas. "Be here then, and you can help me close."

"Great!" Thomas responded. "But…uh…I need you to pay me in advance."

"What's this all about?" Mike asked with a little concern.

There was no one else in the shop at that moment, and since Thomas trusted everyone there, he told them all that had happened.

"That is so sweet of you!" Grace gushed. "I want to be a part of it. I've got thirty bucks to add to the pot."

"I've got twenty I can throw in," Maddie said enthusiastically.

Mike did some quick calculations in his head, then opened the cash drawer and pulled out five twenties.

"Wow! A hundred bucks!" Thomas exclaimed.

"That's your pay plus my donation to the cause," Mike shot back. "Now, how is this going to go down?"

"They need help today," Thomas began excitedly, "and I've been thinking about how to do it! While I'm here with you closing up the shop, somebody needs to take the money and go shopping for them. I was wondering if your wife could do that part."

"Ordinarily I think Penny would love to do something like that," Mike answered, "but she's sick with a cold right now."

"No worries!" Grace spoke up. "I can do it."

"And since I'm not needed here, I can help you," Maddie added.

"That will be fun!" Grace said. "I'll come by here and pick you up when I get off work."

"Perfect!" Thomas exclaimed to G.C. "So you take the money. After you and Maddie buy everything, take it here." Thomas handed her a piece of paper with the family's apartment building's address on it."

"So…do we just buzz their apartment number and have them come get it?"

"No, no, no!" Thomas shot back adamantly. "We can't let them know who's doing this! That's what makes this so fun! Just wait for Mike and me to get there. I've got a plan."

A little after seven that evening, Thomas and Mike spotted the girls in Grace's car parked in front of the targeted apartment building.

"How'd you do?" Thomas asked excitedly. The two girls just pointed to the back seat, which was literally filled with grocery bags.

"Our little pile of money bought all that?"

"Well...I took up a collection at work to add to the pot," Grace said with a smile. "So what's your plan for sneaking in there with all this stuff?"

"Watch," Thomas returned and walked up to the locked front door. Pulling a screwdriver from the tool belt he was wearing, he unscrewed the faceplate of the apartment intercom and pretended to be repairing it. He only had to wait for a few minutes before a tenant arrived, typed in her code on the door lock, and walked in. As she hurriedly entered, the door swung to close behind her. Like lightning, Thomas slapped a piece of tape over the bolt in the door just before it shut. The result was that the dead bolt was blocked, but the electric locking mechanism buzzed as normal.

Thomas allowed the woman time to disappear down the hallway before he smiled to his friends and pulled the front door open.

G.C., Maddie, and Mike quickly jerked open the back doors of the car and began grabbing armloads of grocery bags. Thomas lifted out the remaining ones and led them into the building, remembering to remove the tape from the door lock. They traveled quietly to the third-floor apartment where the family lived.

"Just pile everything in front of this door," Thomas whispered. "Then put this note on top." As he was speaking, he pulled a piece of paper from his pocket and handed it to Mike.

"I have another surprise for them," Grace said, giggling as she drew from her pocket a small envelope that had *To Josh's mom, from Jesus* written on the front.

Thomas gave her a questioning look.

"It's a job opportunity!" she answered in a low voice. "I talked to some people at work and found they desperately need help with filing in the Documents Department. She needs no prior experience and no skills. She could step right into it."

When all the groceries were in front of the door and the notes were set on top, Thomas directed his friends to retreat to the end of the hall to watch Josh and his mom's reactions. Thomas then exited the building, effortlessly climbed the outside, and retraced his steps along the third-floor ledge. Taping another note on the window with the writing facing inward, he rapped loudly on the glass and hurried away.

Josh was gobbling down his third peanut butter and jelly sandwich when he heard the noise. His mother heard it too, and both reached the window at the same time.

"What does the note say, Mom?"

"It says, *Open your front door*," his mother read. Both of them turned and raced excitedly to the door. When Josh jerked it open, the entire entrance was blocked with food.

"OH, MY GOODNESS!" Josh screamed and began jumping up and down when he saw the mountain of groceries.

His mother dropped to her knees and began crying.

"There's another note on top!" Josh exclaimed. "It says, *I love you both, Jesus*! There's an envelope here for you too, Mom."

Still weeping, the woman took it and read the card inside. As she did so, she began to sob.

"What is it, Mom? What is it?"

"Josh! It's a job!"

From the end of the hall, the three friends were all wiping away tears but had large smiles on their faces. They could hear the boy's enthusiastic cheers and the mother's crying words, "Thank you! Thank you, Jesus!"

When Thomas arrived back on the ground, he found his friends standing around Grace's car smiling, hugging, and wiping tears.

"Wasn't that cool?!" Thomas asked excitedly as he walked up.

Grace tried to answer but was still too choked up.

"Yeah," Mike admitted huskily. "It really was!"

"Wow!" Maddie exclaimed with a deep sigh. "That was the most…uh…uh…Jesus-ish thing I've ever done!"

"SEE!" Thomas shot back. "I told you it'd be really fun!"

"I want to do that again!" Maddie said sincerely.

"Me too," Grace squeaked.

"I'd be up for that," Mike agreed.

"Absolutely!" Thomas laughed excitedly. "So let's ask God to show us some of the needs around us. Then we just keep our eyes and ears open to what He wants us to do.

Chapter Thirteen

Working in the Security Administration Office was often stressful for Grace. Mondays were always hard, but this one was particularly bad. Her boss was Devlin Trask, the new city deputy administrator, and to say that he was difficult to work for was a huge understatement. If she didn't need to be there for the Christian underground, she would have quit her job a long time ago.

There was a small mountain of arrest reports on her desk that she had to process. Many of them were arrests of Christians when the police had discovered their secret meetings. What upset Grace the most was that some of the reports documented violence and abuse used by the officers during the arrests. *They aren't even trying to hide it!* she wanted to shout.

In the past Grace had pointed out some of the abuse to her boss. Trask's response was to laugh and tease Grace for being too squeamish, then lecture her on the need to crush these religious rebels so hard that they totally give up the idea of God altogether.

Grace spent the morning dealing with as many of the vile reports as she could until her anger rose to the boiling point. Desperate for a break, she left her desk and walked down the hall to the Records Room. Strolling in, she noticed a new face busily filing forms and records.

"Hey, Margie!" she said cheerfully to the older lady in charge.

"Oh, hello, Grace! It's been three or four days since you've come down to see us."

"I know," Grace returned. "They've been keeping me so busy that I can't seem to get away from my desk.

"I see you have a new worker."

On hearing this, the new filing assistant turned to face the two women. "Yes, we do!" Margie said enthusiastically. "Grace, this is Cheryl Gibbons.

"Cheryl, this is Grace Collins. She's about the only ray of sunshine you'll find in this building."

"Oh, come on, Margie," Grace returned, a little embarrassed. "There are a number of nice people here."

"Not like you, girl!" Margie shot back. She then turned to Cheryl. "You definitely want to get to know Grace. If you ever need help, I can tell you for certain that she will always have your back."

"That's good to know," Cheryl said with a smile as she extended her hand toward Grace.

Grace shook the offered hand warmly. "So how'd you find your way here?" Grace asked with a knowing smile.

"It's the strangest thing," Cheryl began. "I was in desperate need of a job, and out of nowhere I heard about this one. I'm so grateful to Margie for hiring me."

At this point the phone rang, and Margie went to answer it, leaving the two women alone in their conversation.

"Hmm," Grace returned. "It sounds like this job dropped right out of heaven for you."

"Funny you should say that," Cheryl said, looking around to be sure no one else was listening. "I think it did!" She spent the next several minutes briefly and cryptically telling Grace the story of what had happened to her and her son, Josh. "I'm not a person who believes in that stuff, Grace...at least I wasn't. I'm not so sure now. My mother-in-law was a Christian. That's where Josh learned to pray. After my husband died, Josh would stay with her while I worked. When she died, things got a lot harder. Believe it or not, all this great stuff started happening after my son started praying. To tell you the truth, since all this occurred, I'm really interested in finding out more about Jesus."

"I can understand that," Grace answered. "If I had experienced all that, I would be curious as well. You just need to be careful around here who you say those kinds of things to."

"Yeah, I know," Cheryl said with a nod of her head. "They arrest people for that. You aren't going to turn me in, are you?"

"No, Cheryl, I won't turn you in. Just be careful who hears your story."

"Thank you, Grace! Oh, I will be careful…but I still wish I could learn more about Jesus."

"Well, you said everything started happening when your son prayed," Grace said. "Why don't *you* pray and ask Jesus to provide a way for you to learn about Him."

"Hmm," Cheryl said thoughtfully. "You know…I will. I absolutely will."

Grace saw Margie hang up the phone and knew that this part of the conversation needed to end. "It was so good to meet you, Cheryl," Grace said, dismissing herself.

"It was nice meeting you too," Cheryl returned.

"I think I'll stop back by in a day or so," Grace returned, "just to see what kind of answer you get."

Okay, okay! Grace thought to herself as she left the Records Room, *This is one of those things we talked about. Cheryl has another need. Lord, You've told me what You want me to know. Now, what do You want me to do? How do You want to meet Cheryl's need for wanting to know more about Jesus?*

Grace's mind was racing as she hurried back to her desk. She worked feverishly through the pile of reports on her desk, but the whole time she was praying for a plan. At one point her prayers were interrupted by her boss when something didn't go to suit him, and he came storming out of his office and spent the next twenty minutes yelling at everyone he could find.

In spite of that, by the middle of the afternoon, Grace was convinced that she knew exactly what God wanted her to do. But she also knew she was going to need some special help.

Looking through the glass partition and seeing that her boss was consumed with something on his desk, Grace got up and walked over to the coffee station. She fixed one cup of coffee with cream and sugar. She then poured a second cup that she left black. After another nervous glance at her boss, she picked up both cups and hurried down the hallway. She darted quickly through one of the doorways and took the stairs to the bottom floor in the basement. Striding purposefully down the long, dark hallway, she eventually came to a door on the far end. Entering it, she found herself in a small broom-closet of an office where one of the data entry people was busy hovering over his keyboard.

The young man was startled when the cup of black coffee was placed beside him. He smiled pleasantly when he saw who had brought him the hot drink. Pulling his earbuds out of his ears, he picked up the cup. "Thanks, Grace!" he said in a nasally voice. He was a mousey-looking man with dark-rimmed glasses that were taped around the bridge. His name tag said *Oliver J. Meeks.*

"Hey, O.J.," Grace returned with a smile.

"What brings you down into the dungeon?" O.J. asked as he sipped his gift.

"I just needed to get away for a few minutes." She checked the hallway to be sure no one could hear her next words. "That man!" she hissed in a low, angry voice.

"Trask?"

"Yes!" she shot back, still speaking in almost a whisper. "He is such an evil person! I hate the way he treats people. Sometimes I think you've got the best job…hidden down here away from his ranting and raving."

"I agree," Meeks smiled back. "I do have the best job here. Trask and all the other uppity ups don't even know I exist. They think I'm just some nobody nerd who can type…and I like it that way!"

"So did they load you up with a pile of stuff to type in today?" Grace asked.

"They always do. They think it will take me days to type it all in. I finished that pile a couple of hours after they gave it to me."

Grace looked suspiciously at the heaps of documents and forms scattered sloppily over O.J.'s desk.

"I always keep a messy desk so they can't tell what I'm doing," he answered with a mischievous smile.

"So what are you doing?" Grace asked curiously.

"Oh, you know…just pursuing some creative ideas that might help the friends of a certain Jewish carpenter we both know and love."

"Anything you can tell me about?" Grace asked with an excited gleam in her eyes.

"Umm…not yet. It's not quite finished, but I am getting close. You know how it is. The fewer people who know about it, the better. But when I get it done and, if it turns out as good as I think it will, you'll be the first person I tell."

"Well, listen, O.J.," Grace began as she glanced a second time down the hall to sure no one was there. "I've come up with a plan. It probably isn't as big a deal as yours, but I think it's pretty cool. The problem is I need your help to do it. You normally walk to work, isn't that right?"

"Yeah, that's right," O.J. returned curiously. "I walked today."

"Would you be willing to meet me in the garage after work and let me drive you home? I can explain my plan, and you can tell me if you're willing to help."

"Sounds exciting," he said as he pushed his glasses back into place where they had slid down the bridge of his nose. "Could it be that my devious little mind is starting to rub off on you?"

Chapter Fourteen

That evening Grace led the way to her car, and O.J. shuffled meekly behind her, carrying his beat-up backpack. Once they were in the car, Grace began talking: "I'm going to take you home like I promised, but I've been thinking about this whole plan of mine. I've gone over it again and again, and honestly, O.J., I don't think we should do it."

"What do you mean?" O.J. asked, disappointment in his tone.

"Okay," Grace began, "I'm trying to get a package to a friend here at work, but I don't want her to know it came from me. Actually, I don't want her to know it came from anyone here at work. I was going to use you to pretend to be a delivery man and just show up at her door. But then I realized that, since she works here, she might recognize you too, and it's just not worth the risk. So I'll have to put my ol' thinking cap on and figure out some other way to get it to her.

"You haven't met Thomas yet," Grace continued. "I'll try to get him to help me."

"The plan's still on," O.J. returned confidently. "It'll work. There's no need to involve what's-his-name."

"Thomas."

"Right…Thomas," O.J. returned. "You won't need to bring him into all this. I can make this work for you."

"But she might recognize you, and that could really mess things up!"

"I promise you she won't recognize me."

"How can you be so sure?" Grace questioned. "No offense, but you're pretty unique looking."

"*Heh, heh, heh*…I'll take that as a compliment. But I still promise that she won't recognize me. Let's do it."

"I don't know, O.J.…."

"Trust me, Grace. There's stuff about me that you don't know. Your plan will work, and she won't recognize me. I absolutely guarantee it."

His complete confidence was what finally convinced her. Following O.J.'s directions, Grace pulled up to a street corner and parked. As O.J. opened his door, Grace asked, "So you live here?"

"No," the young man returned, "but close to here. From the time I joined the underground, I decided that the less that people knew about me, the better. That's some advice that you should follow as well."

"So, when will you be back to pick me up?"

Grace glanced at her watch. "I should be ready to get you in three quarters of an hour," Grace answered thoughtfully.

"Then in forty-five minutes I will be waiting for you right here," O.J. returned. Spinning on his heel, he quickly disappeared into the dark shadows of a nearby alley.

Grace drove off feeling less confident than her friend.

As night fell, she wove her way through the evening traffic to the part of town that she normally tried to avoid. The reason was that dear friends of hers lived here, and because of the secretive work she was doing, it was important to her that she protect this family. Unfortunately, she needed something from them tonight.

Grace parked several blocks away and exited her car. She deliberately kept to the dark shadows as she hurried through the side streets and alleys until she arrived at a corner flower shop which was closed for the evening. She loitered in the shadow of a nearby building, carefully watching the street and the alley to make sure that she was not being followed. When she was fully convinced that she had not been observed, she stealthily made her way down the dark alley beside the store. A short walk brought her to an insignificant-looking metal side door. She had to knock three different times before she finally got a response.

"Who's there?" she heard a low voice on the other side of the door.

"Your adopted daughter," Grace answered with a smile.

When the door cracked open, a voice gasped and said in a hushed voice, "Grace! Get in here!"

She quickly rushed through the doorway, which was hurriedly shut and locked behind her.

Grace hugged the middle-aged man who let her in. Finally he held her at arm's length and said, "You know you shouldn't be here, but I'm so glad you came! We've missed you so much! Come on up."

Grace was ushered into the upstairs apartment. As soon as she entered, there were squeals of excitement, and she was immediately swarmed with hugs from each family member, which she eagerly returned. Frank and Emily Watkins, along with their two daughters, Sharon and Susan, ran the Midtown Florist Shop. Years ago, Grace's parents had led Frank and Emily to become followers of Jesus Christ, and their families had been close ever since. After her own parents passed away, the Watkins became a second family to Grace.

"So…how's the flower business?" she asked with a mischievous grin.

"BLOOMING!" all four of the Watkins shouted together and laughed at the family joke.

"Seriously, Grace," Frank asked, "what are you doing here?"

"I've been trying to avoid coming to see you in order to protect your family," Grace began. "I wouldn't have come tonight, but I have a real need, and, Frank, you are the only one I know who can help me with it."

"What is it?" Emily asked what they all wanted to know.

"I need a book," Grace said, looking straight at Frank.

"A book," Frank returned.

"Yep."

"Just one?"

"Yes," Grace answered with a nod. "Just one."

Mr. Watkins nodded his understanding and quickly walked into his bedroom. While he was gone, Grace tried to catch up with all that was happening in her friends' lives.

Within a few minutes Frank returned and handed Grace the item. She turned to Mrs. Watkins and asked, "Emily, do you have a way that I could wrap this and make it look like a shipped package?

"We should be able to handle that, shouldn't we, girls?" There was much giggling as Emily and her daughters descended to the back of the flower shop, excited to be a part of Grace's secret plan.

In ten minutes Grace was saying her heartfelt goodbyes and stepping through the door into the alley with her package.

"Do you want me to walk with you to your car?" Frank asked with concern. "I hate to let you go out alone at night...especially in this part of town."

"Thanks for asking, Frank, but I've got this," Grace answered, then smiled and gave him another quick hug. "All of you are the closest thing to family I've got now, so please take good care of yourselves!"

"You too!" Frank returned with feeling. "Grace, we pray for you every day."

"I'm counting on it!" she said as she disappeared into the night.

Without hesitation Grace raced back to her car. Checking her watch, she pulled out and quickly headed back to the rendezvous with her friend.

She made good time as she retraced her path through town. Grace was pleased when she noticed that she was actually a few minutes early, arriving at the agreed-upon location to pick up O.J. She jotted a name and address on the package as she waited.

Just then Grace was startled when suddenly the passenger door jerked opened, and a strange man in a blue uniform hopped in and stared at her.

Chapter Fifteen

The sudden appearance of a uniformed stranger getting into the car with her unnerved Grace so much that she jumped. "Excuse me! What do you think you're doing?!" Grace exclaimed anxiously as she began frantically grabbing for the door handle.

"G.C., calm down! It's just me."

"JUICE?!" Grace was stunned at the transformation. "You're kidding me! Is that really you?"

"Yep, it's me all right," O.J. returned with a big smile. "What do you think?"

"Oh my goodness!" Grace gasped, patting her hand over her heart and still staring at her transformed friend. "You…you look…totally different! What did you do?"

"*He he*…This is one of my disguises. It's a pretty good one, don't you think?"

"But…but you're taller, and your hair is different! You don't even sound like yourself! And…oh my goodness! Your glasses, Juice…Where are your glasses!?"

"Okay, okay…h*ee, hee, hee,*" Juice answered with a chuckle, "I'll explain it to you. It's not magic, Grace. I'm taller because at work I slouch."

"You slouch?" Grace asked with a confused look.

"Yes, I slouch whenever I'm there. I've actually perfected the fine art of slouching. All you've got to do is keep your knees slightly bent, bow your shoulders, and always look down. You can lose five or six inches of height doing that.

"My hair is different because I've slicked it back with hair cream. It looks darker, doesn't it?" All Grace could do was nod her head, dumbfounded.

"When I first applied for my job at the Security Administration, I decided that the office nerd I'm portraying at work should have a nasally voice, so that's how I speak there. I'm using a different voice for my delivery man disguise."

"But how can you get around without your glasses?!" Grace demanded.

"I'm not wearing glasses because I honestly don't need them. They have no prescription in the lenses; they're just clear glass. I use them to hide behind at work. To tell you the truth, they're not even broken. The tape on the bridge is for show, to make my image there more believable.

"This outfit I'm wearing now is another one of my disguises. I thought it made me look more like a delivery man."

"Wow!" Grace said in amazement. "You're right! I would never have recognized you. Honestly, O.J., I'm totally stunned at the change. You look like a completely different person. But why do you do all this?"

"Grace, you of all people should understand. The work we're doing for the persecuted believers is dangerous…really dangerous. We are going against some of the most evil and crafty servants Satan has. Eventually, either we're going to make some mistakes, or they're going to out-think us. When that time comes, I want to be ready. I've come up with multiple escape plans, should I need them, and I have five new identities I can take on at a moment's notice, complete with history and identity papers."

"Wow!" Grace exclaimed. "That must have taken some time!"

"Well, yeah," O.J. returned. "It took some work. But, Grace, what we do is too important. I don't want to just give up if the authorities start tracking us down. If they come after us, what I want to do is to shift directions and keep on doing God's business."

"That's amazing!" Grace answered in a stunned expression. "You've considered this whole thing in much more detail than I have."

"Well, you need to think about it," O.J. returned. "It's definitely something you should plan for. You know good and well that we will not always be able to stay ahead of the authorities. When the time comes for our enemies to catch up with us, it is critically important that we already have our next moves planned out. We've got to outthink them in order to stay ahead. If you want, as soon as you're ready, I can help you come up with a couple of your own new identities."

"Hmm, I should talk with the rest of the team about that as well," Grace said her thoughts out loud.

"Yep," O.J. returned. "*Wise as serpents…*"

"*…but as harmless as doves,*"[6] Grace said, finishing the familiar words of their Master.

When they arrived at Cheryl and her son's apartment building, Grace drove past the entrance and parked around the corner. After explaining her plan to O.J., he nodded his head to acknowledge that he understood. Exiting the car, O.J. took the package and walked to the front door of the building. He pressed the button beside the number for Cheryl's apartment. He was about to press it a second time when he heard a voice over the speaker.

"Yes?"

"I have a package for Cheryl Gibbons at 347 Sparkman Arms Apartments," O. J. returned in a low, official-sounding voice.

"Uh…yes, that's me, but I didn't order anything. Who's it from?"

"It just says that it's from somebody named J.C."

"Hmm…well…"

"Lady, please!" O.J. exclaimed in mock frustration. "I've got other deliveries I need to make!"

"Okay, okay, bring it up," she said as the lock on the front door buzzed open.

A few minutes later Cheryl answered the knock on her door. Before her stood a tall young man in a blue uniform holding a brown package towards her. He had his blue cap pulled down low so that the visor almost

---

[6] Matthew 10:16

completely covered his eyes. "Cheryl Gibbons?' he asked as he looked down at the address.

"Uh...yes."

On hearing this, the young man shoved the package at her and quickly turned to walk away.

"But...uh...what is it?" Cheryl called after his retreating form.

O.J. never stopped walking, and he didn't turn back to face her. "Search me, Lady," the young man called over his shoulder. "I just deliver 'em. I don't open 'em."

As the strange delivery man disappeared down the steps at the end of the hall, Cheryl closed the door and set the package on her table. She was confused and took a moment to study the outside of the package.

"What's in the package, Mom?" Josh asked excitedly when he saw what his mother was looking at.

"I don't know," she returned, still in deep thought. "I didn't order anything. The only writing on it for a return address are the initials J.C."

"J.C.!" Josh gasped. "Maybe it's another gift from Jesus! But I didn't ask for anything. Did you?"

"Actually, I did," Cheryl remembered. "I asked for a way to get to know Jesus better."

"OPEN IT, MOM! OPEN IT!"

Josh's enthusiasm was enough to spur Cheryl into action. The wrapping was quickly torn off, revealing the contents.

"It's a book," Josh said with a little disappointment in his voice.

"No, Josh!" his mother answered with tears streaming down her face. "It's not just a book. Son, it's a Bible!"

Chapter Sixteen

O.J. gave Grace a thumbs up as he climbed back into the car from delivering the Bible.

"You're sure she didn't recognize you?" Grace asked with concern.

"Not a chance," O.J. returned. "I didn't give her any time to get a look at my face. She was too busy checking out the package. It worked like a charm. That was really cool of you to do that for her, by the way."

"It was Thomas who started it all," Grace admitted. "He found out about their needs and got several of us to help Cheryl and her son."

"Thomas…the guy that's been working with you and Egg."

"Yes, that's right," Grace returned. "I keep forgetting that you haven't met him."

"That's fine," O.J. answered. "I don't need to. I appreciate what he does for the Lord, but the less we all know about each other, the better."

"You've got me thinking, O.J.," Grace asked a few moments later. "What should I do to prepare if the authorities discover what we've been up to?"

"First of all, it's not *if* the authorities discover us. It's *when*. You definitely need to create two or three new identities that you can immediately take on if you need them, but I think the first thing you should do is come up with an escape plan."

"Can't I just pack a bag, jump in my car, and drive away?" Grace asked.

"That would be ideal," O. J. returned, "but what if you get discovered at work? What if you're being chased, and you can't get to your car? How will you get out of town without your car if the police are after you? Where will you go? How will you access the supplies you'll need? You will also require places that you can safely go, both inside and outside the city, and hidden caches of emergency supplies or people who can get them for you. You need people you can trust who you can contact in a crisis."

"Do you have all that?" Grace asked in amazement.

"All that and more."

"Oh my!" Grace gasped. "Where do I start?"

"Begin thinking of scenarios where things can go wrong," O.J. explained. "Start with what you would do if your ties to the Christian underground were suddenly exposed at work. If they take you by surprise, there's nothing you can do. You're just caught. But if you get a few minutes' warning, you need to be prepared to completely change your appearance and have preplanned at least two escape routes out of the building."

"How can I change my appearance in just a few minutes?" Grace asked in frustration.

"You won't have a few minutes. You must practice what you are going to do over and over again until you can do it for real in thirty to forty seconds. Keep a small pair of sharp scissors and a small bottle of hair dye with a fake label in your purse at all times. When the time comes, you must get to the ladies' room or some closet as quickly as possible, cut your hair short, get it wet, and pour in the dye. Comb it back while it's still wet, and you can look like a guy. Start wearing a different type of shirt under your work outfit, keep a pair of light-weight pants rolled up in your purse to put on."

"What about my shoes?" Grace blurted out. "I always wear heels to work."

"There are a couple of things you can do to change the appearance of your shoes quickly," O.J. answered. "First, knock the heels off. They're only glued on. Then you can sew some cloth bags to pull on over your shoes that make them look like boots or work shoes. Put elastic in the top edges of the coverings so they won't slide down."

"Where am I supposed to keep the pants and fake shoes?"

"Roll them up and keep them in your purse," came the answer.

"All that stuff won't fit in my purse!"

"Then start carrying a bigger purse!" O.J. shot back. "Grace, figuring this out and adjusting to what it takes to be able to do it quickly and efficiently is the difference between life and death! If you are captured because you aren't prepared, then that's definitely the end of your underground work for God and, maybe, your life."

"Wow!" Grace exclaimed as she took it all in. "There is so much to think about, plan out, and practice."

"Yep," O.J. nodded back, "and that's just if it happens at work. What if you're at your house…or visiting a friend…or out for a walk? You need to prepare all of this for each situation and practice until everything becomes automatic.

"As you think through each scenario, work out at least two escape routes. Figure out a safe place you can go to inside the city and a long term, safer place outside the city. Plan your routes so that you can get to each place as quickly as possible. But staying safe and undetected is better than being fast. When you make your plans, tell yourself that you will have to use them. Our enemies are not stupid. They will eventually figure out who we are and what we're doing. Think of discovery as a certainty, so be ready at a moment's notice to implement your plans. Lastly, Grace, remember, when it's time to act, DON'T HESITATE!"

Grace was up for hours thinking about all that she had heard and working on plans. She knew she needed notes, but she didn't want to leave evidence of what she was doing, so she wrote everything down using the code that she and Egg transmitted their written messages in.

By the time she finally forced herself to go to bed, she realized that there was an enormous amount of work still to be done to be ready. The needs were almost overwhelming! It would take a lot of time to find safe spots and plan out escape routes. She would also have to explore the area outside the city to find some good hiding places and figure out how to stash away some emergency supplies in or near them. If she had to, she would get Thomas to help her find places to hide and to connect with people who could help her in an emergency. Thomas, Egg, and O.G.P. needed to be making their plans as well — if they hadn't already.

Oh, my soul, she said to herself as she lay in bed, trying to slow her brain down enough to go to sleep. *This is going to take weeks! I just hope I have weeks!*

When she realized that fear was gripping her heart, she stopped and did what she should have done hours before. She knelt beside her bed and had a long, passionate talk with her Heavenly Father. At one point she remembered Jesus's words, *Let not your heart be troubled, believe in God, believe also in Me.*[7] That was all the encouragement she needed. Gratefully she expressed all of her fears and worries to her loving and faithful Lord, then gave all of them into His hands. "They're Your fears and worries now, Lord. I fully trust You to handle all of them, and I refuse to pick them up again. You know the future, Father. You know what I will need and what I won't, so I trust You to show me all that I need to know and how to accomplish it. I love you, Lord! In the mighty name of Jesus, Amen."

Now I can sleep, she thought as she gave a big yawn.

---

[7] John 14:1

Chapter Seventeen

The couple stayed in the shadows as they crept cautiously along the dark street. The early moon had set, and there was only one distant streetlight to be concerned about.

The middle-aged man and woman, constantly on the alert, clung to each other as they moved stealthily along. They passed several houses, eventually arriving at a thick hedge bordering a driveway. The man halted and checked the number on the mailbox. Without saying a word, he nodded to the woman and pointed up the drive. They reached the large house and continued to the back.

Suddenly the dark shape of a man confronted them, startling the couple. "Who comes?" the figure hissed in the lowest of whispers.

"Two...for Him," the man murmured in response.

The dark figure disappeared for a moment, but quickly returned with a second person. Suddenly the man felt a hand grab his and tug him forward. The couple were led through the blackness along the back yard of the house. No words were spoken, but the man and his wife could tell that they were walking downhill. Apparently the house was built on a slope and was tucked up against thick woods that came near to the back of the house.

Unknown to them, the couple and their guide were being observed covertly through a night vision scope by a prone figure in the forest seventy-five yards away. The watcher was hidden in the blackness of the evening woods as the cross hairs of his infrared rifle scope followed the unsuspecting newcomers.

"Two more," the sniper hissed faintly into a microphone attached to his helmet strap.

"Copy that," a voice crackled in his earpiece. "That makes fifteen, plus the two outside."

When the couple reached the far end of the house, their guide lightly tapped twice on a low wooden door built into the brick foundation. It quickly opened, and the couple were ushered inside. The earthy smell and slight dampness made it clear to the newcomers that they were in the crawlspace under the house, but because the house was built on a slope, the 'crawlspace' was close to ten feet tall on the end where they were.

When the door closed behind them, a small flame burst from a lighter. "Come, friends," the man holding the light whispered. He was tall and had a short beard and friendly eyes. Turning, he led them along the dirt floor, past cinderblock pilings supporting the house.

They had only taken a few steps when several flickering candles ahead of them revealed a group of twelve people sitting in a circle on wooden boxes and cinderblocks.

Nervous smiles and nods came from those in the group when they recognized the newcomers. In the background the heater's blower fan rumbled as a precaution to cover the sound of their voices.

"Sorry we're so late," the man who had just arrived said in a whisper.

"It's understandable," a middle-aged man returned. "We all have to be careful.

"We just finished our prayers. Do you have something to add?"

"We got word," the woman with the man spoke up, "that our daughter's two children are very sick, but because they are known in their town as followers of the Master, none of the doctors will treat them. They desperately need our prayers."

"There are no believing doctors or nurses where they are?" the leader asked.

"They live in Georgetown," came the answer, and everyone nodded understandingly.

The leader of the small gathering of believers began crying out to God in a low voice, asking for help and healing for the mentioned children and for God's blessing on His followers there.

"Could a medical team slip into Georgetown to hold a clinic for the brethren?" one of the group asked when the prayer ended. "I know they've done that before."

"It's more difficult now," the leader returned. "For the past month the secret police have really been cracking down on house churches. A number of our people have been arrested."

Many in the group nodded that this was not news to them.

"What are we going to do?" another asked.

"We're going to be faithful," the leader returned confidently, "and keep praying. The Lord promised us that following Him would lead to persecution but that faithful endurance provides great blessings.[8] Our brothers and sisters have been facing this for two thousand years. With or without persecution, our work for Jesus doesn't change. Be encouraged by the words of our Lord, *Be faithful unto death, and I will give you the crown of life.*[9]

"Let's spend some time worshiping God," the leader continued, "then we'll have anyone who has a word from the Lord share it with the rest of us."

The leader started a praise song that they all knew, but instead of singing, the group whispered the words together in unison. Other songs were suggested and whispered together in praise to God. Every believer was encouraged by the peace and courage they

---

[8] Matthew 24:9-13
[9] Revelation 2:10

received from this period of genuine adoration to their all-powerful God and His Son, Jesus Christ.

After almost forty minutes of worship, the leader held up his hand and asked, "Does anyone have a word from the Lord for the rest of us?"

Just then the door splintered and crashed inward. Helmeted figures in black jump suits rushed in with their weapons at the ready.

"NO ONE MOVE! YOU'RE ALL UNDER ARREST!"

Chapter Eighteen

The young man carrying a skateboard under his arm knocked on the oak door and stuck his head in the office. "You wanted to see me, Dr. Robertson?"

"Sit down, Thomas, and close the door," the well-dressed man said gruffly.

Thomas Westcott crossed the room, propped his board beside one of the nice armchairs directly in front of Dr. Edwin Robertson's imposing desk, and sat down.

"Thank you for coming," Robertson began. "As one of the Educational Administrators of the New Self Church, I am responsible for the instructive and spiritual needs of our members. I know that you have only been a member a short time, and there are some things you need to be aware of.

"First and foremost, since we are the only officially approved church, the government is deeply concerned that we educate you in principles of good citizenship. Good church members are good citizens. Remember that."

Thomas nodded his head uninterestedly.

"It has come to my attention that you have been sleeping through some of your good citizenship and government loyalty classes. You cannot develop good citizenship by simply dreaming about it, Thomas."

Thomas squirmed in his seat.

"I have asked you here today to help you catch up on some of the important teachings that you have missed because of your naps," Dr. Robertson began as his eyes seemed to bore a hole into Thomas's soul. "There's a church policy handbook in front of you. Pick it up and turn to page fifteen. You will follow along as I go over some of the points you may have missed."

Opening the booklet to the mentioned page, Thomas found a hand-written note in the margins. He read, *Our egg-headed friend said I could trust you. Disregard what I'm saying and read this.* Grateful to ignore Dr. Robertson's droning lecture, Thomas read further. *Be careful what you say*, the note warned. *They suspect me of being friendly to the underground church movement, and I'm certain this room is bugged.*

Last week government agents raided a house church across town. They arrested seventeen of our 'friends' and bulldozed the house down. Eight of the friends associated with them managed to avoid the police and are hiding in a safe house, afraid to return to their homes. I have collected some money to help care for them, but it's too dangerous for me to take it to them. I know you've risked a lot for Him before, and I hate to ask you again, but our friends are in desperate need. If you are willing to take the money to them, then ask me if I'm through with you yet. If you are unable to be my courier, tell me that you are sorry for falling asleep in class.

After a moment of prayerful deliberation, Thomas interrupted Dr. Robertson, "I'm sorry, sir, but are you about through with me?"

"No, I am NOT through with you, Mr. Westcott!" Dr. Robertson growled. "Turn to page thirty-three."

At that place in the book Thomas found another note telling him where to find the money and make the delivery. *My address is penciled at the top of this page,* he read. *The address where the money is to be taken is penciled below it. Memorize them both...don't write them down. Enter my back yard by climbing the fence in the rear of the house. I will leave the small door in the rear of the garage unlocked tonight. You will find the gift under the front bumper of my car. BE VERY CAREFUL! I believe my house is under surveillance.*

PS: Take this handbook with you and destroy the notes.

After leaving the meeting with Dr. Robertson, Thomas's mind was racing. *Let's see,* he thought to himself as he walked down the steps of the huge church building. *I need to get something to eat and get some rest. But first and most importantly I need to get some people praying, and that means I need a cup of tea!*

Slipping the handbook into his jacket pocket, Thomas dropped the skateboard he carried, stepped on, and zipped off for the Cup o' Joy Coffee Shop. There were three people sitting in the small dining area when he arrived. Mike Schuster recognized Thomas's voice when he ordered his tea. He knew this was an odd time for Thomas to be in the shop, so Mike gave his friend a questioning look. Seeing the curious expression on Mike's face, Thomas glanced around to make sure no one was watching. Then without saying a word, Thomas brought the tips of his fingers together in a symbol of prayer.

Mike nodded his understanding and reached into the refrigerator beside him, pulling out an egg and holding it so that only his friend could see. The look on Mike's face revealed to Thomas the question he was being asked.

Thomas gave a simple nod to let his friend know that he was asking for prayers for a project he was working on for the underground.

Realizing the seriousness of Thomas's request, Mike knelt down behind the counter so that only Thomas could see him, and he put his fingers together to assure his friend that sincere prayers would be offered.

Hours later Thomas, wearing a dark jacket and black jeans, sat quietly in the bushes watching for movement in the deepening shadows around the Robertson's yard. It had been fully night for over an hour. He shivered slightly, both from the slight chill in the air and from excitement. He had seen a black SUV parked at the end of the block but had observed no one in the car, nor had he seen anyone moving around the neighborhood as he scouted the area earlier.

Keeping to the shadows, Thomas quietly slipped over the fence, crossed the yard, and slid inside the unlocked rear door of the garage. He easily found the bundle of cash right where Dr. Robertson's note said it would be and placed it inside his shirt.

A faint sound just outside the door alerted him, and he looked quickly for a place to hide. A few moments later, the rear door burst open, and two agents rushed in with flashlights and guns in their hands.

"He's hiding," one snapped. "Search for him." As they began looking, a small pebble clicked softly at the far end of the garage near the large front door.

"He's behind the rear of the car," one whispered. "You go around that side, and I'll take this side." They moved cautiously to the back of the vehicle. Finding no one, they both bent down to look underneath.

As they did so, Thomas dropped from the rafters at the other end of the garage and leapt through the back door. By the time the agents jerked back up, Thomas was closing the door behind him. Hurriedly working their way back around the car and to the door, the agents yanked it open. As they did so, two large, full garbage cans, one stacked on top of the other, came crashing in on them where Thomas had leaned them against the door. When they finally got out of the garage, God's holy ninja was clearing the back fence.

"Quick! Get to the car!"

Thomas ran swiftly up the alley, but he was still fifty yards from the end when, with a screech of tires, the black SUV wheeled into the lane and accelerated towards him. Thomas grabbed the top of a wooden privacy fence to his left and easily launched himself over it just as the car slid to a stop behind him. He heard a shot ring out as he dropped to the ground on the other side and felt wood splinters pepper the back of his neck. The young courier sprinted across the yard and quickly cleared the fence at the front. Without a pause he raced across the street and jumped the fence of another yard. As he darted across this property, a large black dog snarled and charged after him. He had just cleared the back fence as the snapping jaws lunged for his legs. Landing in another alley, Thomas made his way toward the closest end.

The black SUV raced down streets and alleys searching for their prey. Turning down yet one more alley, they almost ran over an old homeless man bent over his cane, hobbling along.

"Get out of the way, old man!" one of the agents yelled as they roared by. The old derelict stumbled out of the way as the car raced past, shaking his cane at the disappearing vehicle.

As the car rounded the corner and drove away, Thomas straightened up and tossed aside the stick he had used as a cane and pulled off the nasty cap he had found run over in the road. Taking off the green jacket he wore, he turned it right side out, revealing its dark exterior. He quickly slipped it back on.

Jogging to the end of the alley, he traveled a short block to the old business district. The young courier ran to the rear of the nearest building and climbed up onto a wooden awning above the rear door. He stepped onto a second-floor window ledge and was able to reach the down spout, which he quickly scaled to the roof. From there, three stories above the street, Thomas was able to see the people and cars moving below. He noticed that the black SUV was parked along this avenue. As he watched, another black car pulled up beside the first one. After a few moments they both drove away, heading back into the neighborhood that Thomas just left. He carefully worked his way across the tops of the buildings until he had arrived at the far end of the block. Cautiously he descended to the street and disappeared into the night.

Just after eight-thirty the next morning, there was a knock on the side door of a white framed house on Hemmings Street. A middle-aged lady cautiously answered the knock. She saw a haggard-looking young man facing away from the door.

"Yes?" the lady questioned.

The young man kept his eyes and his face averted from the lady as he held out a package to her and announced, "Special delivery."

"I don't understand," she responded. "What's this?"

"It's help for some needy friends," the young man responded, still looking away.

"Oh!" she said with a little start as she suddenly realized what the package contained. Then, as she understood that he averted his gaze so that he could not recognize her if he were caught, she quickly looked away from him as well. "Thank you so much!" she continued. "We have been...uh...hoping for this."

"You're welcome," he responded, "but thank our Boss. He's the one who sent it.

"I need to leave now," the young man continued. "The friends send you love and greetings in the Boss's name. Please tell our friends in need that they are not forgotten."

"Did you have much trouble getting this to us?" the lady asked with concern.

The young man paused for a moment. "None to speak of," he finally answered over his shoulder.

"May He bless you," she said quickly as the young man walked away.

The blessing caused Thomas to pause. He nodded his head in acceptance. He needed as many of those as he could get.

"And you as well," he called over his shoulder as he continued on his way.

Chapter Nineteen

Two days later the bell over the door of the Cup O' Joy coffee house rang, and owner Mike Schuster looked up to see who had come in.

"Hey, Mikey ol' boy! I need some hot leaf juice!"

"HOT *LEAF* JUICE?!" Mike shot back. "I should kick you outta here, Thomas, for insulting my teas. I'm already upset at you!"

Thomas Westcott cut his eyes over to Maddie, who was standing behind the front counter, and saw that she was scowling and nodding her head in agreement with Mike.

"Why are you upset with me?" Thomas asked, still smiling. "What did I do?"

"Because every morning that we're open, you're in here like clockwork. You're a fixture."

"Yep," Maddie agreed firmly.

"We expect you."

"Yep," the girl repeated.

"It's part of what makes the day…uh, right," Mike continued.

Thomas looked at the girl behind the counter and, with folded arms and a stern look, she nodded her agreement.

"But yesterday," Mike continued, "you didn't bother to show up, and our universe fell apart."

"It couldn't have been that bad," Thomas laughed.

"Are you kidding me?!" Mike shot back. "After you coming in here two days ago asking for..." Suddenly Mike stopped, and his eyes searched the shop. Assuring himself that no one else was there, he continued. "After you coming in here two days ago asking us to pray for one of your escapades, then not coming in yesterday, we were pretty concerned! The least you could have done was let us know you were okay!"

"I'm...uh, sort of...uh...doing that now," Thomas answered sheepishly.

"A day late is not good enough!" Mike shot back. "It shows no consideration for people who care about you!"

"Also, I had your cup of green tea ready and waiting for you," Maddie added, "but you didn't come in to get it. Nothing went right after that."

"I'm sorry, Maddie," Thomas returned sincerely when he realized that they had wasted a cup of tea on him. "I'll pay you for it."

"No need," the girl answered with a smile. "I'm just glad you're okay. When it was clear you weren't coming, I sipped on your tea through the day. But you need to understand how really nice of me that was because I don't even like green tea. It's bitter."

"See, Madds, that's why you need to add a little milk to it," Thomas advised.

"BUT THAT RUINS IT!" Mike exploded at them both.

"Mike, you're too much of a purist," Thomas laughed.

"And *you* need to learn how to drink tea…AND communicate with your friends!" Mike shot back as he turned to make Thomas a cup of hot green tea.

"By the way, where were you yesterday?"

"I was up all Sunday night and most of Monday working on the…uh…project. When I finally got back to my apartment, I was exhausted. I needed to catch up on my beauty sleep."

Mike turned and looked at his friend. "Hmm…It didn't work.

"Oh, and another thing! If you haven't done so already," Mike added, "you should let our special friends know that you're okay. They've been concerned about you as well."

"Okay, okay!" Thomas returned. "Point taken! I'll do that today…as soon as I get a chance."

After he paid for and received his tea, Thomas gave Maddie a wink and walked to the small prep station. He added the usual amount of honey to his drink and then, with a big smile at Mike, poured in some milk.

"YOU'RE RUINING IT!"

With an annoying chuckle Thomas replaced the lid on his cup, waved to his friends, and walked out the door.

His tea was half gone when he arrived back at the tall apartment building where he lived. The superintendent was sweeping the front steps as Thomas walked up.

"I wondered if you were gonna' show up for work today. I was worried about you since the note on your door yesterday said you felt really tired and were resting up. I pounded on your door this morning, but you were already gone."

"It was a bit of a rough day yesterday, and I was a little later than normal this morning getting out of bed," was Thomas's answer. "I felt better when I finally got up, but then I had to go get my wakeup cup." As he said this, he held up his tea. "Don't worry, Boss, I'm clocking in as soon as I get my coveralls on."

"Well, once you do, you can finish this," the man said, tossing Thomas the broom. "Also, Mrs. Pierce in four twenty-six said her sink is clogged, and the Jeffers in two sixteen said their closet door is stuck. Get those done, and I'll probably have a much longer list for you."

Thomas took another swallow from his cup, gave his boss a cocky smile, and announced, "I'll handle it! Elvis is in the building!"

Thomas walked the three flights up to his apartment, changed into his overalls, put on his tool belt, and returned to the first floor to clock in.

Three hours and swept steps, an unclogged drain, a repaired closet door, and a replaced light switch later, Thomas slipped to the upper floor, unlocked the access to the roof, and, after closing the door behind him, ascended the steps.

He loved coming up here. It was peaceful, had a great view of the city, and was swept with breezes that carried lots of fresh air. He cautiously scanned the roof and the surrounding buildings to be sure he was alone and not being watched. Taking one more deep breath, Thomas walked over to the apartment building's tall television antenna attached to the four-foot-square and three-foot-high metal ventilation box located in the center of the flat roof.

Thomas studied the wire that ran down the tower from the pipe containing the laser transmitter, then carefully studied the small box the wire ran into to be sure that it had not been tampered with. He slipped a tiny earpiece with a mini microphone into one ear and, holding the audio wire, stooped down beside the small box. Rotating one of the screw heads on the front revealed a hidden audio port. Plugging in the headset, Thomas pressed another screw head on the box and began to speak. "This is Forty-five checking in."

There was a long pause before a very anxious voice sounded in his earpiece. "D...DUDE, WHERE HAVE YOU BEEN? WE'RE WORRIED SICK ABOUT YOU!"

"It's all good," Thomas returned. "There was no reason to worry. The delivery was made, but it was all the way across town. Making that trip on foot while dodging suspicious-looking cars took a lot out of me. I needed to rest, so as soon as I made it back, I crashed at my apartment. I'm sorry I was out of touch. Is anything going on?"

"Absolutely!" the voice crackled back. "We need you to come in. O.G.P. has a cool project to discuss with you."

"When?" Thomas responded.

"Three up-two" came the answer.

"Got it! Out!"

Thomas quickly disconnected his earphone's audio cord and shoved it in his pocket. He just as quickly moved the false screw head back over the audio port and, after checking to be sure that everything appeared as it should, headed down the steps.

Let's see...Three, he thought to himself as he recalled Egg's cryptic message. *Sunday, Monday, Tuesday...that's today. Up-two...that's the time.* Thomas started to look at his watch, then remembered that Egg always used Jewish time. *The Jewish day starts at six pm,* he reminded himself, *so up two from that is eight pm. Okay, good...that's after dark.*

Thomas stopped briefly on the first landing he came to. Pulling a piece of paper out of his pocket, he studied the formidable-looking list of repairs that needed his attention. "Hmmm," he finally said, "I should have plenty to keep me busy until eight."

Chapter Twenty

*W*ho *is she?* Thomas wondered as he made his way along the roofs and alleys to his meeting at Egg's. *According to her...and Egg, she's wealthy and apparently very smart. But what does O.G.P. stand for? Ophelia Gertrude Potts? Not Ophelia...nobody is named Ophelia. How about Octavia? No, that sounds like some Roman goddess. But her name could be Olive. She looks kind of like an Olive. What other 'O' names do girls have? How about Olivia? Yeah, that's probably it...Olivia something Phillips... or Peters or Powell or Poindexter or...Ploppindorf. Well, whatever her name is, I'm just glad the Lord's got her. Most people would have used all that hidden money on themselves instead of on God's business. Thank you, Lord, for O.G.P.*

Thomas trotted across the top of the roof of Egg's building. Stopping at the right rear corner, he scanned the two alleys below as well as the surrounding buildings. Seeing nothing suspicious, Thomas lowered himself over the edge and, using the bricks protruding from the corner, nimbly descended to the rear window of Egg's apartment. He was pleased to find the window open and ready for him.

"Did anyone follow you?" Egg asked when Thomas entered the computer room.

"Well, all the pigeons are sleeping right now," Thomas returned cockily, "so maybe a bat or two might have, but I'm on good terms with most of them."

Egg spun around and glared at him.

"Look, Egg, I know how important it is to protect you and this place. I take a lot of precautions all the time but especially when I travel here. If I was ever even remotely suspicious that someone was watching me, I wouldn't come."

Egg seemed satisfied with his answer and spun around to face his computer screen. Thomas was just about to take a curious look over his friend's shoulder when O.G.P. walked through the front door.

"Do you live in this building?" Thomas asked curiously. "I thought you had to buzz at the front door to get in."

"She has a key," Egg answered over his shoulder.

"I don't have a key," Thomas returned with hurt in his voice.

"You don't need a key."

"So what's this project of yours, Oliv…uh…O.G.P.

"Egg has spent a number of days searching through the Security Administration's computer programs," she responded, "and he found something very interesting."

"Really?" Thomas expressed his curiosity as he turned to face their brilliant friend.

"Among a lot of other very interesting things," Egg began, "I found where they organize, schedule, and record the raids they make on the house churches."

"You mean as in knowing when and where they will strike?" Thomas asked hopefully.

"Precisely that!" Egg smiled back.

"The problem is," O.G.P. continued, "that they don't post the final complete information in the computer until the order to launch the raid is given."

"Wow, that won't give us much time to warn them," Thomas said his thoughts out loud.

"We can't use phones or radios," O.G.P. said, "because the government monitors all of that."

"We will have to try to send someone to warn them," Egg said over his shoulder.

"And by *someone*, you mean *me*," Thomas returned.

"That's why you're here, Forty-five," O.G.P. announced. "We think a raid is planned for some time tonight."

"There's usually a flurry of activity on the computer when a raid is imminent," Egg explained.

"And you've seen that today?" Thomas asked.

"Yes, I have. The team has been listed and the vehicles identified. All that is lacking is the location and the confirmation of the order to initiate the raid."

"But what if it's across town?" Thomas asked with concern.

"Then we can't do anything to help," O.G.P. answered. "But if it's on this side of town, I can get you close in my car. Then you'll have to do what you do the rest of the way."

"HERE IT IS!" Egg exclaimed, leaning into his computer terminal. "Six ninety-nine Westmoreland Avenue." His fingers flew across the keyboard, then suddenly he announced, "THAT'S WESTMORELAND PARK! GO! GO!"

"But that's a big park!" Thomas shot back. "Where will I find them?"

"We'll ask God to lead you," O.G.P. said as she ran for the door. "NOW COME ON!"

They took the elevator to the ground floor and rushed out of the door. In a few minutes they were racing toward the park in O.G.P.'s car.

"There it is up ahead!" she announced urgently, then added, "Lord, please show Forty-five where they are and protect them all!"

"AMEN!" Thomas cried as he jumped out of the door before the car had come to a complete stop.

Sprinting into the dark park, only a few streetlamps illuminated the sidewalk. Thomas didn't think the friends of Jesus would meet in the open, so he turned and sprinted through the brush to his right. He raced up a sparsely wooded hill, stopping occasionally to listen for voices. Suddenly he heard multiple cars squealing to a stop back on the street behind him. He was out of time.

Throwing back his head, Thomas yelled as loudly as he could, "FRIENDS OF JESUS, RUN! THE POLICE ARE HERE!" He then turned and ran through the woods in the opposite direction from the sounds of the vehicles. Behind him he could hear loud voices and shouting.

Thomas had entered the park on the northeast corner. After several minutes of running, he came out on the northwest corner. Looking over his left shoulder, Thomas spotted several figures rushing out of the park and darting into the surrounding night shadows. "Thank you, Lord!" Thomas whispered the prayer when he spotted people hurrying away. Taking a deep breath to calm himself, he began walking across the street and away from the park. *Please don't let the police find them, Lord,* he prayed as he walked.

"HEY, YOU!" he heard an authoritative voice behind him.

And don't let them catch me either! Thomas added to his prayer as he bolted and sprinted away.

The chase didn't last very long. Racing down an alley, Thomas came to a tall, chain-link fence. Without slowing down, he leapt as high as he could and was able to grab the top edge of the barrier. He pulled himself effortlessly over the top and continued running down the backstreet.

With his helmet and riot gear, the policeman was unable to keep up with the young fugitive and had to stop at the wall of welded wire. Panting and breathing hard, the officer snarled in anger as he pounded the chain-link fence at losing his victim.

As soon as he sprinted out of the alley, Thomas made the turn and quickly scaled the wall of a three-story building beside him. He realized that, though he might be in the clear right now, he had been chased enough to know that his situation could change in an instant. In Thomas's experience, he was aware that his pursuers were devious and had radios. To escape these guys, it was clear to him that he needed to be sneaky as well.

Once on the roof, Thomas moved quickly but quietly to the front corner where he could see both the street and the alley. Stealthily glancing over the ledge, he spotted the police officer who had been chasing him wave to another uniformed agent nearby.

Thomas slipped off his backpack and pulled out his listening device. Putting in the ear buds and switching on the electronic mechanism, Thomas pointed it at the two officers below him.

"Did you lose him?"

"He jumped a fence that I couldn't get over with my equipment. He thinks he got away, but he's only one street over. You run south and swing around to the next block. I'll go north and do the same thing, and we'll trap him between us."

"Okay, but just to be sure, radio in and have all available patrol cars cover the next three streets to the east."

"Right!"

Thomas had heard enough. By the time he packed up his gear, the two officers had split up and were disappearing around both ends of the block. He quickly descended the corner of the building and raced into the shadows to the west.

Three hours later Thomas was able to slip unnoticed into his apartment building. He remembered Mike's lecture and thought about reporting in to Egg as he wearily climbed the stairs, but when he reached his floor, he stopped. *I'm beat!* He thought to himself. *God used all of us to do some good for His people tonight, and that's a win for His kingdom. I'm glad to be a part of it, but I'm exhausted. Egg and O.G.P. can hear my report about it tomorrow. My bed is yelling to me right now. Egg can yell at me tomorrow. I desperately need some sleep!*

"Besides," Thomas said out loud, "how can they expect me to keep all my secret agentness skills honed without proper rest." Thomas gave a big yawn and headed determinedly to his apartment and, most importantly, his bed. "Us secret agents must get our sleep."

Chapter Twenty-One

The fact that Devlin Trask had no friends did not concern him in the least. In fact, he preferred not having any. The way he looked at it, friends only got in the way and complicated his plans. The fact that no one wanted to be his friend just made his life simpler. He was focused on the future of his career in the political party, and there was no room in his life for anyone or anything that might get in his way.

He had clawed and fawned his way up through the ranks of the security forces until he had been made captain. Continuing his bootlicking career plan as well as a little personal blackmail against those in his way, Trask had eventually found himself in the enviable position of Deputy Chief Administrator for the City of Grantham. He looked the part too. He wore dark suits and had sharp, intense features. It took an entire can of hairspray each week to keep his jet-black hair impeccably combed. He also made it a priority to keep his sinister-looking goatee always well-trimmed. Having spent hours in front of the mirror perfecting the appearance he wanted, Trask had crafted a look that was designed to intimidate.

He had only held this position a short time, but he already had enough dirt on his boss, the City Administrator, to get her kicked out whenever he was ready. But before he could make his move, he wanted to create a reputation for himself in the city. His appetite for more power was insatiable, but he was also patient. When the time was right for Trask to get rid of his rival and the party council met to choose the next administrator, Trask wanted to be sure that his name was first on their list. He had decided that the best way for him to build the reputation he needed was to absolutely crush the Christian problem and their secret meetings. That plan had worked well for him in his last posting, so he felt sure it would be successful in Grantham also.

Unfortunately for his ambitious plans, Trask was discovering that his strategy wasn't as easy in the big city. When he first began, he had been successful in targeting believers in Jesus and made many arrests. But over time, things had changed. The Christians were learning and adapting to Trask's plans. It was becoming increasingly harder to find them, and when they did get an address for a secret meeting, it infuriated him that many times someone would get a warning to them just before the police could arrive.

"...and when we do catch them and shut down their criminal gatherings, ten more suddenly spring up," Trask snarled to his assistant. "They're like...like...ROACHES!"

At that moment there was a knock on his office door. Through the glass he saw an attractive young woman holding a stack of papers. Trask waved her in. "What do you need, Grace?"

"I have these papers for you to sign, sir."

Grace set the documents down on his desk, and the Deputy Administrator began hurriedly scribbling his signature on them.

"What were we talking about?" Trask asked his assistant distractedly. "Oh yes, the Christian problem."

"You'll get them, sir!" his young assistant fawned.

"Not if we keep doing the same things, Nash!" Trask snapped back. "The old ways aren't working! We've got to be smarter...sneakier."

"More devious, sir?"

"Exactly," Trask returned with a sneer. "And I think I've figured out a way to do it."

As he said this, the Deputy Administrator looked out the large window of his private office and watched as a black-uniformed officer roughly dragged a young woman past the desks and cubicles. Trask eagerly waved at the officer through the glass, indicating that he was to bring the woman to him. He quickly finished signing the reports and dismissed Grace with a gesture.

Shoving the captive woman into a chair in front of the desk, the officer handed Trask a handful of papers that he greedily snatched up and quickly read through, searching for the information he wanted.

As G.C. stepped out of the office, she studied the woman who had just been brought in. Her hair was messy, and her clothes were disheveled from being roughly handled.

Grace put the signed papers on her desk and walked to the coffee station that Trask had ordered to be set up just outside his office. As she pretended to check the coffee machine and to slowly fill her cup, she lingered beside the window, hoping to catch some of the conversation in the Deputy Administrator's office.

Devlin Trask smiled and chuckled to himself as he read through the report. When he finished, he looked at the woman sitting across from him, spotting a bruise forming on her cheek. "Danita Jefferson," Trask said with a sneer, "you know you really shouldn't give the officers any trouble. It always leads to pain...ALWAYS!" As he angrily yelled this last word, Trask came out of his chair, slammed his hands on his desk, and lunged toward the terrified woman.

Seeing his victim's startled jerk and the fearful trembling, Trask knew he had the girl right where he wanted her.

G.C. jumped as well when she heard the shout. *He is such a cruel and evil man!* She said to herself as she hovered beside her boss's office.

"GRACE!"

Fear exploded in her stomach as G.C. heard Trask scream her name. She tried to hide the fear with a fake smile as she looked at her boss through the glass, praying that her spying had not been discovered.

"COFFEE!"

Relieved, the smiling G.C. nodded and began fixing a cup the way he liked it. She then reentered the office and placed it on Trask's desk. Grateful to escape detection, Grace quickly hurried out the door.

It would be too risky and look suspicious for her to hang around near Trask's office any longer to attempt to hear more of the conversation. But rather than

146

returning to her desk, she darted down the hallway and into the women's restroom. She cautiously examined the room and was relieved to find that no one else was there. Stepping into the farthest stall and latching the door, she pulled off her right shoe. Carefully lifting the lining, she removed the folded-up piece of paper she kept there. She quietly spread it out on the wall and scanned the writing.

The paper was covered with coded notes and bits of information that she had picked up during the day from conversations in the office or from simply keeping her ears open to what was being said around her. The sole reason Grace worked in the building was to listen and learn what the enemies of Christ were planning against His people. Any information, no matter how insignificant it might seem, could be critical to what they were trying to do to help the believers. It must be recorded, and she had to make sure that it got to those who needed it, even if it cost her dearly.

Later this evening when she returned to her apartment, Grace would secretly check in with Egg and relay all of the information. But for now, additional interesting observations needed to be added to the notes.

What she had just heard could be extremely useful to Egg and O.G.P. as they made their plans. Snatching a pen from her skirt pocket, Grace wrote in coded shorthand all that she had heard of the conversation in her boss's office.

Whoever that young woman is, Grace thought to herself, *I'd certainly hate to be her right now!*

Chapter Twenty-Two

"**W**ell, well, Ms. Jefferson," Trask said when he finished studying the records of the trembling woman sitting across from him, "black market activities, eh? It seems you and your parents have broken quite a few laws. That's too bad...too bad. But that's why we created our labor camps. We needed a secure place to put criminals like you and your family. I think your parents will fit right in there, don't you?"

"Oh, please, sir," Danita Jefferson pleaded tearfully, "my parents are too old for that, and my mother is sick! The only reason we sold on the black market was to afford my mother's medicine! My parents wouldn't last a week! They'll *die* in a labor camp!"

"Yes...yes, they will," Trask returned with no emotion. "They will die there...unless *you* do something to save them."

"Me?"

"Yes, you, Ms. Jefferson," Trask countered. "Your parents will die in a labor camp unless you step up."

"Step up? What do you mean? What can I do?"

"I have a job I need you to do for me," Trask began, closing the trap. "With your skills at lying and deception, this job should be right up your alley."

"What kind of a job?" Danita asked nervously.

"Oh, it will be a perfect fit for someone with your criminal mind," Trask returned with a grin. "And if you do it, not only will I let your parents return home, but I will even make sure your mother gets her medicine. Is that something you might be interested in?"

Danita nodded cautiously. "What do you want me to do?"

"Let me explain my problem," Trask began with a sinister smile. "We're having trouble finding all the Christian groups in this area. They're like snakes. They're sneaky and conniving. I need you to be just as sneaky. Your job is to identify these radicals, infiltrate their groups, and find where and when they meet. Then you are to bring that information to me. It's as simple as that. Do you understand?"

"But how will I find them?"

"We are fairly certain that some of them frequently attend the government's New Self Church. Can you believe the arrogance of these people, trying to hide their illegal activities directly under our noses? We believe they contact each other there and pass information to the different secret groups.

"That's where you will start. Go to the meetings. Listen and watch, and when you find someone you think might be one of them, then convince them to accept you into their group. As soon as you have information, I want to hear about it! You will report back to me here each week...sooner if you have a lead. As long as I think you are making progress, I will leave your parents alone. But if I think you are stringing me along, Ms. Jefferson, then *all* of you go to the labor camps! You will never see your parents again! AND YOU WILL HAVE NO ONE TO BLAME BUT YOURSELF!"

Thomas was grateful for the opportunities he was getting to help the persecuted believers, but there were aspects to his secret work that he didn't like at all. One of those things was having to regularly attend the government's New Self Church. The sermons and the classes were nothing but government propaganda couched in religious-sounding terms. Occasionally while he was there someone would slip him information to get to Egg, which made all the boredom and frustration almost worth it.

Today was one of those occasions. His assignment for this particular meeting was to make contact with one of their agents carrying important information. He was told that he would be able to identify the person by the flowery shirt he would be wearing. Unfortunately for Thomas, he had spotted six flowery shirts in the crowd milling around in the large foyer between classes and the assembly.

Apparently, flowery shirts are a thing, Thomas murmured frustratingly to himself. *Who knew?*

He pushed closer to each individual until he could see their feet. Finally he spotted one wearing red sneakers. Stepping beside him, Thomas bumped shoulders with the person and in a friendly manner said, "I hope the lesson today is as good as the one two weeks ago."

"Two weeks?" the fellow in the flowery shirt asked without looking at Thomas.

"Sorry," Thomas answered with his code phrase, "One week ago."

Satisfied that Thomas was the legitimate courier he had been sent to meet, the man in the flowery shirt nodded and extended his hand to Thomas. As Thomas shook the offered hand, he felt the piece of paper being passed to him. As he turned to walk away, he carefully slipped the message into his pocket.

Mission accomplished, he said smugly to himself as he and the rest of the crowd were herded into the large assembly hall for the service. *Now all I have to do is endure this speech. Lord, help me!*

The service had just been dismissed, and Thomas was feeling rather pleased with himself and his skills as a 'master spy.' He quickly made his way out of the building and was walking with others along the sidewalk when he felt someone bump into him and grab his arm. When he looked down, he saw a scared-looking young woman desperately hanging onto him.

"Please help me!" she hissed in an urgent whisper. "I'm in trouble! I think the secret police are after me!"

"Uh…Do I know you?" Thomas asked suspiciously.

"No…no, you don't," the woman shot back, "but I think I've got a real problem, and I need your help!"

"Why would the police be after you?" Thomas asked, looking back over his shoulder. Sure enough, he saw a big man in a dark suit and sunglasses pushing through the crowd towards them.

"I think one of them spotted my Bible," she answered. As she said this, she reached into her jacket pocket and pulled out part of a worn black book that said *Holy Bible*.

"WHAT?!" Thomas gasped urgently under his breath. "YOU'RE CARRYING A BIBLE AROUND WITH YOU? HAVE YOU COMPLETELY LOST YOUR MIND?"

"I know...I know...it was dumb," she whispered back defensively. "But it's important to me, and I've always carried it. I really need you to help me!"

"Good night, Irene!" Thomas hissed to himself in frustration and took another look behind them. It was clear that the police detective was heading their way.

"Come on!" Thomas said resolutely. Grabbing the woman's arm, he pulled her hurriedly through the crowd toward an alley on their right. He glanced back as they made the turn and saw the man in the suit trying to forcefully push his way through the mass of people in order to follow them.

Thomas urgently pulled the woman down the alley as fast as she could run, all the time desperately searching for a way of escape. Just ahead of them he saw several garbage cans sitting against a large green dumpster. Thomas raced for them.

The security agent was having some difficulty forcing his way through the thick crowd leaving the government's church. When he finally broke free, he rushed to the alley down which his quarry had disappeared. As he turned into the damp and dirty opening, he could see Thomas running out the other end.

"Oh, stink!" the slightly overweight police agent spat in frustration. Running as fast as he could in his suit, he raced after the retreating figure, trying to reach the alley exit before the escapee could get completely away.

The red-faced agent was wheezing hard when he arrived at the far end of the alley. He put his hands on his knees and sucked in huge gulps of air to try to catch his breath. After his third lungful, he stood and quickly looked for the man he was following. He spotted him two-thirds of the way down the block, running like a deer.

"ARRGH!" he growled loudly in disgust. "I don't get paid enough to do this!" Taking several more deep gasps of air, the weary undercover policeman determinedly hurried after his prey.

Chapter Twenty-Three

$\mathbf{A}$ short time later Thomas descended a drainpipe on the side of a building and landed in the alley near the big green dumpster. Cautiously creeping over to one of the smaller garbage cans, he jerked off the lid, which resulted in a startled scream from inside.

"You okay?" Thomas asked as he reached down to help the girl out of the can.

"I've been better!" she snapped. "Why did I have to hide in one of the little cans?"

"Because I thought he might check the big dumpster."

"Well, it stunk in there! And now I stink!"

"But he didn't catch you," Thomas said with a smile as she exited the smelly can.

"I guess the least I can do is thank you," the young woman said, sticking out her hand. "I'm Linda Winters."

"Uh...Hi," Thomas returned, giving her hand a tentative shake.

"And you are?" the girl pressed.

"I am...uh...late," Thomas shot back evasively and started to leave.

"Wait! What do I do now?" the woman asked urgently.

"Go home and...take a bath," Thomas returned with a sniff. "There's a bus stop up at the corner," he said over his shoulder as he hurried toward the opposite end of the alley.

"NO...WAIT!" the woman cried and lunged after him, but Thomas had already sprinted away. By the time she reached the end of the alley, her rescuer was nowhere in sight. With an angry stomp of her foot, she huffed and whirled around to find the bus stop.

Later that afternoon another tense meeting took place in Devlin Trask's office. "What do you have for me, Danita?" Trask asked, glaring angrily at the young woman who trembled in the chair across from him. "And let's hope for your parent's sake that it's more substantial than your last report."

"The last trick worked, sir!" she confessed eagerly. "I've finally made contact with someone!"

"Who is it?" Trask pressed. "Give me a name!"

"He wouldn't tell me his name."

"WHAT?" Trask screamed as he slammed his fist onto his desk.

"But I can find out!" Danita exclaimed in terror. "He's wary of me, sir. I...I just need to contact him again and try to build his trust. Just give me some more time!"

Trask took a deep breath and tapped his chin thoughtfully. Finally he said, "All right, Ms. Jefferson, I'll give you a few more days. I have something big going on anyway. But I...and your parents...are expecting results from you, do you understand?"

"Yes, sir!" she answered with an eager nod of her head. "Yes, I do!"

Thomas watched curiously from the couch as Egg and O.G.P. engaged in a private but intense discussion beside Egg's computers. "So is all this about that message I brought you?" Thomas asked.

Both of his companions stopped talking and looked at him.

"What's going on? It's obviously something important. And both of you know that you're going to ask me to do some 'death-defying deeds of daring do' because of it, so you should go ahead and just tell me."

O.G.P. nodded at Egg, and he began the explanation. "With the increased persecution and the intense scrutiny of the police, the churches have been reporting for some time that the followers of Jesus here in Grantham are getting discouraged. During times of intense persecution, discouragement can have a harmful effect on the faith of some. It's gotten so bad that Christians in other areas are hearing about it and are concerned for us."

"So much so," O.G.P. added, "that we just got word that Gabriel, a powerful Bible teacher and great leader of the believers, is coming here to meet with the house churches specifically to encourage the brothers and sisters."

"Whoa!" Thomas exclaimed. "With the police cracking down hard on the churches here, that could be really dangerous for this guy Gabriel! The police would love to get their hands on someone like him. Is that really his name?"

"No," Egg answered. "Just like us, our church leaders and teachers have taken on code names to hide their movements and activities from our enemies. And yes, the police would give anything to catch him. That's where we come in."

"It is up to us to set up the meetings with the different house churches around the city," O.G.P. explained.

"So who's going to be responsible for actually getting him to and from each of these meetings safely?" Thomas asked with raised eyebrows.

Both Egg and O.G.P. just smiled at Thomas.

"I figured as much."

"Forty-five, you will be the contact person," Egg said reassuringly, "but we will all be working with you to make sure you know what to do. G.C., Juice, and a few other agents will be helping us make sure this happens the right way."

"When is this Gabriel guy showing up?" Thomas asked, trying to grasp all that was being asked of him.

"The note you brought says that he's supposed to be here in ten days," Egg said. "That means we have a lot of people to contact and a lot of serious plans to make. I will let you talk to Mike Schuster about what's happening. It's going to be dangerous, but tell him that we will need him to come up with a safe place for Gabriel to stay while he's in the city. Thomas, whatever Mike comes up with, it's going to be up to you to figure out a way to get Gabriel in and out of there without being noticed."

Ten days later, in the middle of the night, a dark-colored van pulled up to an old barn behind a farmhouse almost twenty miles outside of Grantham. When the doors of the barn slid part-way open, two people scrambled out of the van and rushed inside. Shortly afterwards the vehicle pulled away from the farm, turned onto the highway, and headed back the way it had come.

Just after sunrise a beat-up delivery truck arrived at the front of the barn. On the side of the truck was painted *Big Tom's Elegant Junk*. Two large men in coveralls jumped out and knocked on the farmhouse door. A man in work clothes answered and directed the two workmen to the barn. When the big doors were slid opened, the farmer led the others inside. A few minutes later the two men came out carrying a large box marked *tools*. After storing it in their truck, the two men went back inside and came out with another box marked *antiques*.

After handing the farmer an envelope, each man shook his hand, climbed back into their truck, and headed toward Grantham.

It took them less than thirty minutes to get back to the city, but it required another twenty minutes of weaving through city traffic and streets to work their way back to the shop. They pulled through an alley and parked in the rear of Big Tom's. After being sure that the alley was empty, the men swiftly carried both heavy boxes into the back of the building.

Chapter Twenty-Four

Thomas had to change his morning routine as soon as he was informed that Gabriel was coming. For the last several days, instead of heading to the Cup O' Joy as he usually did first thing each morning, he hurried to the roof and contacted Egg on the laser transmitter to see if there was any news. On this day he finally received the message he had been anticipating.

"The package has arrived, Forty-five," Egg's voice crackled through the headset, "and is ready for pickup."

"Is the location the same as we discussed?" Thomas asked.

"Yes," Egg returned. "Let the inn keeper know what's happening on your way to pick up the package."

"Got it...Out," Thomas answered and shut down the transmitter.

The inn keeper, Thomas said to himself as he left the roof. *That would be Mike. It looks like I get my morning cup of tea after all.*

Thomas made his way determinedly to the Cup O' Joy only a few blocks away. He was anxious to get there, but he didn't want to attract attention to himself, so he tried to look like he wasn't hurrying.

He walked through the front door of the tea shop and expected to hear Mike's usual welcome, but instead it was a female voice that called to him.

"Well, good morning! I've been hoping to see you again!"

Thomas stopped and looked for the source of the greeting. To his right, seated at one of the few tables in the shop, was the woman he had helped escape from the police days earlier.

"Oh, uh...hey," Thomas answered cautiously. He walked past her to the counter, hoping to pass on a secret message to Mike, but the woman got up and followed him.

"You left before I had a chance to thank you," she said as she stood beside him.

"Uh...green tea, please," Thomas said to Maddie at the counter, then turned to face the young woman.

"There's no need to thank me," he said.

"Oh, you're just being modest. Of course there is. You really helped me out. You didn't do my clothes any good, but you kept me from getting arrested."

"Shush!" Thomas snapped softly, looking around. "Don't say stuff like that! You don't know who's listening!"

"Oh...right, right!" the woman returned contritely. "Well, I'm just glad I ran into you, because I wanted to talk to you again."

Thomas paid for his tea, picked up the cup, and followed the woman back to her table, all the time racking his brain to come up with a plan to get a message to Mike.

Just as they reached the table and the woman sat down, it came to him. Taking a sip of his tea, he stopped and jerked around angrily to face the counter. "HEY, WHAT ARE YOU TRYIN' TO PULL HERE?!"

"What's wrong?" Maddie asked from behind the counter, caught off guard by Thomas's anger.

"THIS TEA IS WEAK AS WATER! I WANT TO SEE THE MANAGER RIGHT NOW!" Thomas yelled as he marched back to the counter.

Mike realized that something wasn't right and quickly rushed to the counter to see what Thomas was up to. "What seems to be the problem, sir?" Mike asked.

"It's this stuff that's supposed to be tea!" Thomas snapped angrily. "It tastes like water!" He pulled the lid off and moved the cup and himself up closer to Mike. "Just look at it! It looks like water too!"

As Mike leaned closer to look into the cup, Thomas whispered, "I'll be bringing the package to you today."

"I understand, sir," Mike answered loudly enough for all to hear, "the customer's always right. I'll make you a new cup of tea."

"Good!" Thomas barked. "Just make sure you put some tea in it this time." He then walked back to sit at the table where the woman waited for him.

"Wow!" she said with a smile. "You're sure grumpy in the morning."

"I guess that was kind of rude," Thomas admitted. "Things haven't gone the way I expected them to today, and I'm a little irritated. I'll try to remember to give them a bigger tip next time.

"Now, why do you need to talk to me?"

"Just so you know, you're still being rude," the woman returned with the unchanged smile on her face. "Do you remember my name?" The response she got was a blank stare from Thomas.

"It's Linda…Linda Winters. When we met the first time, I told you that I was new in the area and that I didn't have very many friends. Then you helped save me from the police."

"Yes," Thomas returned, "I remember all that."

"Well, I still don't have many friends here, and like it or not, I've decided that you are going to be one of them. So what is your name?"

Thomas gave a sigh and finally said, "You can call me T."

Just then Maddie walked up and said "Here's your fresh cup of tea, Thomas."

With a grimace, he took the cup and thanked her.

"So it's Thomas?" Linda declared with a victorious smile. "Thomas what?"

"Just Thomas or T," he returned.

"Are you so famous that you don't use a last name?" Linda teased.

"Maybe," Thomas returned evasively, "or maybe I'm an orphan and never had one, in which case, all your probing questions could be hurting my feelings."

Linda began laughing when she heard his answer. "That's pretty lame," Linda returned, still laughing. "Listen, I understand. These are dangerous times, and you have to be careful. I'll just call you Thomas, and you can call me Linda…at least until we know each other better."

"Sounds great, Lisa."

"LINDA!"

"Right! Linda!" Thomas corrected as he stood up, "but I've got to go to work."

"Where do you work?" the young woman probed, rising to her feet.

"I…uh…I'm a repairman, and I've got some stuff I need to do." Thomas began walking for the door, and Linda followed.

"So do you work around here?" Linda asked as she trailed him out the door.

"Well, I…uh…work in different places… wherever I have a job."

It was clear to Thomas that Linda was going to stay with him, peppering him with questions as long as she could. He didn't want to be mean, but he really needed to get away from her so he could go meet Gabriel. As they walked, he decided to go on the offensive.

"You said you were new in the area," Thomas said, trying to turn the conversation away from himself. "Have you found a job yet?"

"Oh…uh…well, I…uh…was in sales, but that job got put on hold. Right now I'm…uh…doing some temporary work until I find something better."

Thomas asked a few more questions, buying time until they arrived at his apartment building.

"I've enjoyed getting to know you, Linda."

"Good, you remembered!"

"Yeah," Thomas smiled, "I'll try to do better, but I have some work to do at this building, so I need to go."

"Okay," Linda quickly added, "how about we..." but before she could finish her sentence, Thomas sprinted up the steps and disappeared into the building.

Thomas dropped his half empty cup into a trash can on one of the landings as he sprinted to the roof. Once there, he ran to the rear of the building and scanned the alley below. Seeing no one, he slipped over the edge at the corner and, using the cornices and protrusions from the bricks and stonework, he made his way unseen to the ground.

Chapter Twenty-Five

Thomas quickly followed the path he had planned through the city, arriving at the two-story building that housed Big Tom's Elegant Junk. A buzzer sounded when he walked through the front door.

The shop was absolutely crammed with antiques, odd memorabilia, and, as the name implied, just plain junk. He carefully made his way past a sign that said *You break it, you bought it* and through a narrow walkway between various and sundry items for sale until he arrived at the front desk. A middle-aged woman sat at a computer terminal playing solitaire and sipping from a very large, insulated mug.

"Can I help you?" the woman asked without looking up from her game.

"Yes," Thomas answered, looking away from her. "I'm here to pick up a package for Eggsworth."

On hearing the name, the woman suddenly looked up, then just as quickly looked away. "Uh…Yes, Eggsworth! Those packages did arrive."

"Packages?" Thomas questioned.

"Yes," the woman returned. "Unexpectedly, two were shipped. They're in the back. Follow me, please."

167

She led Thomas through a door behind the desk into a rear workshop. They walked up to a man in coveralls, who was standing by a workbench trying to fix a broken chair.

"This is Mr. Eggsworth," the woman announced. "He's here for the packages."

The man nodded, and the woman left to return to the front desk. Without saying a word to Thomas, the man walked over to a side wall and, pressing a hidden latch, pulled open a secret door. "Gentlemen, come out," the workman called quietly.

Thomas saw two men step out of the darkness. One appeared to be in his fifties and the other noticeably older. The younger one carried a backpack.

"This is Mr. Eggsworth," the workman said, introducing Thomas to the others. "He will be your guide while you are here."

The older of the two men stepped up to Thomas with a confident smile, stuck out a wrinkled hand, and said, "Mr. Eggsworth, I am known as Gabriel, and this is my assistant Silas."

"It's an honor to meet you," Thomas answered nervously as he shook each of their hands. "We weren't expecting two of you."

"I'm sorry about that," Gabriel returned, "but I'm not as young as I used to be and find that I now need someone to assist me. I hope that won't be a problem."

"There may be some added difficulties, but we will all just have to deal with them as they come," Thomas said honestly. "If you are both ready to go, then let me carry the pack, and I'll lead you to where you will be staying."

"It would be best if you exit through the front door like you came in," the workman said to Thomas. "I'll take our two friends out the back and lead them up the alley. Once you leave the store, turn left, go to the next street, turn left again, and I will have them waiting for you at the end of the alleyway." Thomas nodded and headed back to the front of the store.

Almost an hour later Thomas led his two tired charges toward the front of the Cup O' Joy. Stopping just before they reached the shop, Thomas had Gabriel and Silas wait near the corner as he eased up to one of the windows and peeked in. Thomas gave an annoyed sigh when he saw Linda sitting at one of the tables, sipping on a coffee. Hurrying back to the other two, he motioned them to follow him and led them down the alley next to the building.

When they reached the back door of the coffee shop, Thomas knocked softly. He had to repeat the knock three more times before Mike heard it and opened the door. Seeing the two men with Thomas caused him to raise his eyebrows. In response to Mike's look of stunned surprise, Thomas just shrugged his shoulders.

Mike quickly waved them all in and led them up the back stairs to his private apartment above the shop. After introductions were made and the situation was explained, Mike introduced the men to his wife.

"It's not what we prepared for, but we'll make it work, gentlemen," Mike said. "The accommodations will be a little crowded, but we'll make you as comfortable as we can."

"I'm sure Silas and I will be fine," Gabriel answered with a smile. "We are just appreciative for all you're doing for us."

"And speaking for all the believers here," Mike returned genuinely, "we are grateful that you've come. It's so encouraging to know that we haven't been forgotten in our difficulties.

"Silas," Mike questioned suspiciously as he faced his second guest, "what will you be wanting to accomplish while you're here, and what can we do to assist you?"

"My job here is twofold," Silas answered with a smile. "The teacher will be first to admit that his memory isn't what it used to be. I've been assisting him for so long that he now wants me with him as a sort-of spare brain. I have heard and transcribed his lessons so many times that I'm able to offer subtle prompting when his mind occasionally struggles to find the right information."

"My friend is too modest," Gabriel said with a smile. "Without him, I would be incapable of continuing my work."

"You said your work was twofold," Mike prompted Silas again.

"Oh, yes," Silas returned. "As they did in the book of Acts, the teacher and some of the other leaders believe that it is important to document how God is working among His people during these times of persecution. Future generations need to know the details of God's faithfulness as well as the courage and perseverance of the followers of Jesus during this challenging period. That's where I come in. My second job is to document our experiences here, changing the names and locations, of course." To emphasize his point, Silas reached into the backpack and pulled out a notebook.

"Aren't you concerned that the contents of that book might fall into the wrong hands?" Mike asked with concern.

Silas quickly flipped it open to reveal the contents. "As you can see, it's written in coded symbols, numbers, and letters, and I'm the only one who can read it."

"Be that as it may," Mike returned with the same look of concern, "I think it would be best if you don't take it with you when you and Gabriel visit the house churches."

Silas looked less than convinced by Mike's words until Gabriel spoke up.

"Our friend here has a point, Silas," the older teacher said, placing a hand on his companion's arm. "I think it might be wise not to carry your notes with us when we go out. You will have to rely on that wonderful memory of yours and record your observations later."

Silas nodded that he would comply with his teacher's request.

Turning to Mike, Gabriel asked, "When will we get to meet with the believers?"

"One group meets tonight, and we have you scheduled to join them," Mike answered. "It'll be late, so you and Silas should have time to rest. Our friend Thomas will guide you there and get you back here when the meeting's over. If you want to take a nap, that should be fine. We'll have you up and ready to go before you need to leave."

While Gabriel made himself comfortable in the Schuster's second bedroom and Silas collapsed on the couch in the living room, Mike took Thomas into the kitchen and went over the details of where he would be taking the men that evening. "Thomas," Mike said with concern, "you know that your job is going to be more than twice as difficult to slip *two* people into these meetings unnoticed."

His friend nodded his understanding.

"Do you need me to go with you?"

"No! Absolutely not, Mike!"

"But, Thomas, this is not what we expected. With having to account for Silas, we must rethink all of our plans."

"It'll be okay," Thomas returned confidently.

"How can you be so sure?" Mike shot back. "I can't believe they did this without letting us know in time to account for the extra person. Whoever put this together clearly has no idea of the increased danger for you. In a way I feel kind of responsible for you being in this situation, and I want to do something to help you."

"I deeply appreciate your concern, my friend," Thomas answered, "but the responsibility and the added risk is mine...and theirs! Unless absolutely necessary, I insist that no one else be involved. It's true that this is a kink in our plans, but God knew this was going to happen. I am totally convinced that He is way ahead of us on this. He's already made his plans — we just have to figure out what they are."

Chapter Twenty-Six

At ten o'clock that evening, Thomas was at the side door of Mike's coffee shop picking up his two charges. Staying in the shadows, Thomas led them to the park nearby and hurried through it. Once on the other side, they met O.G.P. with her car. Quickly entering the vehicle, she drove them across town, dropping them off in an older section. A long walk down a back street with a couple of turns thrown in brought the three men to an old house in the middle of a block of rundown stores and a derelict gas station. All the windows in the front of the house were black, and the place seemed abandoned, but Thomas led them through the dark shadows to the rear. Knocking twice on a weathered, cellar entrance resulted in the old door being pushed open. "Come in quickly!" a voice hissed urgently from the darkness.

Gabriel and Silas descended the steps. When they looked back to see if Thomas was following, he said, "Go ahead with your meeting. I'm going to scout around a bit."

Grateful for the extra security, the man closed the door and joined his two guests at the bottom of the steps. Flipping on his flashlight, their surroundings were suddenly illuminated.

He led them along a twisting hallway that opened into a meeting room under the front of the house where almost twenty believers sat on blankets on the floor.

"Greetings, friends!" one of the group said cheerfully in a low voice as Gabriel and Silas entered. "We've been worshiping the Lord as we waited for you!"

"Well, don't stop now," Gabriel returned cheerfully. "I can't think of a better way to start our time together than worshiping the One Who loves us the best."

When the cellar door closed, Thomas slid into the shadows surrounding the run-down building, beginning a careful and quiet reconnaissance of the area. He was committed to protecting the two men, as well as the other believers, and wanted to make sure they were safe.

Detecting nothing suspicious in the immediate area, he expanded his search. Sticking to the dark shadows, he decided to circle the block. He hadn't even gotten to the first corner when he heard the faint crunch of gravel under tires behind him. Jumping into the recess of a boarded-up doorway of an abandoned building, he stole a secretive glance back down the street. As he stared into the shadows, he saw something that caused the hairs on the back of his neck to stand on end. A black SUV with its lights off was just creeping out of an alley near the building where the church meeting was taking place.

At first Thomas felt the urgent desire to sneak back quickly and warn everyone, but as he observed the two heads in the car, he noticed that they seemed to show no particular interest in the dilapidated building where the believers were. Deeply concerned at the nearness of the secret police, he started to panic and cried out in his heart. *Lord, this isn't good! Why are the police here?! I REALLY NEED YOUR HELP!*

Suddenly Thomas remembered a conversation that he had with Mike during one of their Bible study times. "Thomas, when things aren't going well, don't panic. God is always with you. He is not only the God Who sees and hears you; He is also the God Who speaks. In my experience He doesn't usually answer "why" questions, so just ask Him what He wants you to know about the situation and what He wants you to do."

Thomas took a deep breath to calm his heart and tried again. *Okay, Lord, I know that You are with me and You are aware of what's happening with these police agents. So, Lord, what do You want me to know?*

As Thomas stood there observing the dark car from a half a block away, he suddenly became aware of the word *listen*. His eyes grew wide as he remembered the sound magnification device he kept in his backpack. After pulling it out, putting in the ear buds, and flipping it on, he eased the device around the edge of the doorway and pointed it at the car.

"How long do we wait?" one officer asked.

"Let's give it more time," came the answer. "Our spy said that he believed a meeting of the Christians was happening tonight somewhere in this area."

"He couldn't tell us anymore than that?" the first one asked.

"No, that's all we've got. So we sit here and watch for anything or anyone suspicious. Just be patient and keep your eyes open. If they're here, we'll get them."

As Thomas listened, he asked the Lord another question. *You've told me what I need to know, Lord. So now what do I need to do?*

Just then the thought seemed to come to him, *They're looking for something suspicious. Give it to them.*

Placing the listening device in his pack and slipping it onto his shoulders, Thomas took a deep breath and stepped out of his hiding spot. He began walking in the direction of the dark police vehicle. Suddenly he stopped and stared at the car. Just then the car's lights flipped on, and it shot out of the alley and turned towards him.

Thomas smiled to himself when he saw that the agents had taken the bait. He quickly sprinted down the street away from the rapidly approaching car, leading them away from the meeting house. Just as the car reached the running figure, Thomas made a quick turn and darted down another alley on his right. Slamming on his brakes, his squealing tires smoking, the driver had to throw the car into reverse and smoke his tires again to steer their vehicle into the alley.

Ordinarily Thomas would have taken that opportunity to lose his pursuers, but this time he wanted to lead them as far away from the actual meeting place as possible. When he reached the end of the alleyway, Thomas paused long enough for the police in the car to spot him before he darted to the left down a new street.

When the police car swung around the corner in pursuit, they spotted their quarry halfway down the block scaling an eight-foot-tall metal fence around a school playground. The car slid to a stop beside the fence, but Thomas was already halfway across the large, grassy area as he raced to the other side.

Once again the driver stomped on the gas and sent the car roaring down the street. It slid sideways as he cut the wheel and launched down a bordering street to reach the other side of the playground. As they drew near, one of the officers spotted the runner as he raced out of the park, crossed directly in front of them, and sprinted into an old cemetery surrounded by an eight-foot-high stone wall.

"We got him!" the officer on the passenger's side cried as they slid up to the entrance of the graveyard. Leaping out of the car and drawing his service weapon, he yelled, "I'll chase him! You get to the back gate, and we'll have him trapped!"

The car raced away as the officer on foot ran through the arched, stone entrance.

When Thomas entered the cemetery, he ran deeper in but always angled to his left. The officer spotted the running figure in the moonlight and tried to take a shot at him, but Thomas was moving too quickly in and around the large gravestones. Racing in pursuit, the savvy officer meant to push the runner toward his waiting partner while always staying between their victim and the front gate.

Thomas knew what was waiting for him at the back gate, so while he kept running toward the rear, he also kept angling to his left. When he finally drew near to the left side wall of the old cemetery, Thomas decided that it was time to lose his pursuers.

Just then he heard a cry from behind. "HALT RIGHT THERE, OR I'LL SHOOT!"

Without slowing down, Thomas leapt to the top of a large headstone and in one movement sprang from it over the top of the stone wall. As soon as he hit the ground and was out of sight of his pursuer, Thomas slid to stop, and shot back the opposite direction. As he raced away, he could hear the radios of the two officers crackling as the frustrated agents tried to figure out where their victim had gone.

Running as hard as he could, Thomas raced down the street and darted into a dark alley. Leaping up, he grabbed a metal downspout on the corner of the three-story brick building and was standing on the roof in less than a minute. From there he was able to watch as the officers in the black SUV searched the surrounding blocks. When he felt they were far enough away, Thomas descended the corner of the building and cautiously made his way back to where the secret Christian meeting was taking place.

Thank you, Lord, for Your faithfulness, Thomas prayed with a smile as he slipped through the shadows.

Chapter Twenty-Seven

After an extended time of whispered singing and prayers, the leader of the house church introduced Gabriel to the others, unaware of the drama taking place outside their meeting house.

"Dear friends," the older teacher began, "it is our greatest honor to be with you this evening...you, who through the privilege of suffering for our Lord, have proven the purity and sincerity of your faith in Jesus Christ, our King. The apostle Paul himself, in encouraging our brothers and sisters so long ago, said...uh, somewhere in Acts, *Through many tribulations we must enter the kingdom of God.*"

"Acts fourteen, verse twenty-two," Silas added with a smile.

"Yes, of course. Thank you, my friend," Gabriel said, placing his hand on Silas's shoulder.

The older teacher went on to remind them of example after example from the Scriptures of the faithful followers of Jesus and the suffering they willingly endured for the love of the Lord.

"Keep your hope firmly fixed on Jesus Christ and the promises He and the Father have made to us!"

Gabriel encouraged. "The Lord said, *I will never fail you or forsake you.*[10] Jesus also said, *I go and prepare a place for you. And if I go and prepare a place for you, I will come again, and receive you to Myself; that where I am, there you may be also.*[11] Those are promises, my dear friends…promises from God the Father and His Son Jesus Christ. When you have nothing else, you always have the promises of God! No enemy, not even Satan himself, can take God's promises away from us! And when God makes a promise, He is going to keep it because the word of God tells us that it is impossible for God to lie…"

"Hebrews six, verse eighteen," Silas inserted.

"Oh…uh…yes!" the teacher agreed gratefully. "And since it is impossible for God to lie, when He and His Son make us promises, you can absolutely trust that They will always, always keep them! When you cannot trust in your circumstances or even in those around you, you can always trust in God.

"The church in Smyrna that is mentioned in the book of Revelation was suffering greatly from persecution, and our Lord's words of encouragement to them was, *Do not…uh…*"

"*Do not fear what you are about to suffer,*" Silas prompted.

"Yes, yes," Gabriel agreed, grateful for the reminder. "*Be faithful unto death, and I will give you the crown of life!*"

"Revelation two, verse ten," Silas said with a smile.

---

[10] Hebrew 13:5
[11] John 14:3

"I can say with utmost confidence, my friends," Gabriel continued, "that God absolutely delights in each one of His followers! He has made us His children and His heirs! All that the Father has given His Son Jesus has also been given to us who believe in His Son! Think about that carefully, my friends. Through our relationship with Jesus Christ, God has given us peace, even in our trials, because He promises to never fail or forsake us.[12] He also promises to work all things, including our hardships, together for good![13]

"Jesus loved us enough to give up everything He possessed for us. May the knowledge of the amazing love that God has for you motivate such love in your hearts that you are willing to offer up everything you have for Him! I want everyone here to know for certain that whatever you give up for God because of your love for Him and His Son Jesus Christ will never be wasted!"

Gabriel and Silas then spent the next hour talking with the Christians and encouraging them. Silas was especially interested in learning their individual stories of how their faith helped them deal with the suffering they were facing.

After more prayer, the meeting finally broke up. They found Thomas waiting for them in the dark shadows near the entrance to the cellar.

"All clear?" the leader asked when he saw Thomas step out of the darkness.

---

[12] Hebrew 13:5
[13] Romans 8:28

"All clear, now." he whispered back. "There was a patrol car cruising the area. They got word through their spies that Christians were meeting nearby, but I led them away. You have a leak in your security you need to address. I'll take my two and leave now, if that's all right."

Gabriel and Silas were slowed in trying to reach Thomas due to all the hugs they received on their way out.

Later that night, safely back in the Schuster's flat, Gabriel dropped into bed, exhausted. Though very tired, Silas stayed up for another hour and wrote feverishly in his notebook all that he could remember from the meeting.

The next day at noon, Thomas had the two teachers on a street corner just in time to be picked up by the vehicle Mike occasionally used for their van church. The large vehicle was almost full when Thomas and the two visitors stepped in. Many of the believers were taking their lunch hours from work to be there. In order to get them back to their jobs in time, the meeting was shortened.

When the mobile fellowship ended, Thomas exited with the two teachers and led them in a roundabout way back to the Schuster's flat. Mike informed the men that their next meeting was that evening. Gabriel immediately excused himself to take a nap while Silas worked on his notebook.

Mike spent some time with Thomas, making sure he knew where they would be heading that evening and the best route to take to get there.

Having quite a list of repairs to get done, Thomas excused himself and rushed back to his apartment building. He pushed himself, and it took the whole afternoon, but he managed to get everything checked off his list just in time to head back to Mike's to pick up the teachers.

Gotcha', Danita Jefferson said to herself as she spotted Thomas rushing out of his apartment building that evening. Desperate to escape the intense pressure Trask was putting on her to make progress, she had spent the last three days going back and forth to the places she knew Thomas frequented. She was standing in the shadows of a nearby building when she spotted her quarry rushing out. Stepping out of the dark shadows, she hurried to follow Thomas.

He's headed to the coffee shop, she said to herself after they covered two blocks, *but why would he go there? It's closed now.*

As they drew near to the Cup O' Joy, Danita saw Thomas duck down the alley beside it. *Okay, he's not going to the coffee shop. He's just cutting through the alley.*

She had worked hard not to be noticed. The fact that Thomas kept looking back over his shoulder made that much more difficult. To keep Thomas from spotting her, Danita decided that she would run around the block and catch Thomas as he came out the other side.

It took her longer than she had anticipated to circle the block, but as she was hurrying toward the alley, she spotted Thomas walking towards her with two men. She pulled her knitted cap down lower on her head and quickly joined a small group of people looking in the windows of the shops on the opposite side of the street.

Danita watched Thomas's reflection in the window as he and the others passed.

Who are those guys with him? she wondered.

She kept her distance as she followed the three men for six blocks. She thought she had been spotted because Thomas made a number of turns down streets and up alleys. Finally she realized that he was just being careful. *Something important is going on,* she concluded and determined not to lose them.

Eventually Thomas led his two friends to an all-night diner and took them inside. Danita found a shadowy nook beside a building across the street and watched them through the diner's large front windows.

What are you doing, Thomas? Danita asked in her mind as she studied the situation. *You came a long, sneaky way just to get coffee.*

She left her hiding place and walked further down the street to get an idea of what was around here. Just then she noticed a couple of black SUVs parked near the end of the block. She hurried up to the nearest one and knocked on the window.

The window lowered, and a gruff voice snarled, "What do you want?"

"What are the police doing here?" she asked bluntly.

"Listen, sweetheart," the officer snarled back, "we're the ones who ask the questions, not you!"

"You better get outta here, princess," the officer's partner growled, "or we'll run you in."

"Listen to me," Danita shot back angrily. "I'm on a special undercover assignment for Deputy Administrator Trask. I've tracked some people he's very interested in to that diner over there, and I need to know why the police are here at the same time!"

"Trask, huh? We'll see about that," the officer huffed as he reached for his radio. "And if the boss don't know you, then you, little lady, are getting' a free trip downtown to have a nice talk with him."

Thirty seconds later a very humbled police officer handed the microphone of his radio to the young woman at his window. "What do you have for me, Danita?" Trask's voice crackled over the speaker.

"I followed the fellow I've been watching and two others to this location and found several of your officers already here on a stake out. Can you tell me what's going on?"

"We got word that a bunch of Christians were going to meet tonight in a building near where you're at. My officers are in position and are about ready to move in and make the arrests."

"Sir," Danita said urgently into the microphone, "I need you to wait. I think the people I'm following are here for that meeting, but they haven't gone in yet. They are sitting in a diner nearby watching."

"Hand the mic back to Officer Driggers," Trask ordered.

"Driggers?"

"Yes, sir."

"Nobody is to make a move until the woman says so. Make sure everyone understands."

"Yes, sir."

"And Driggers?"

"Yes sir?"

"If anything goes wrong, I want that woman brought to me at once!"

"Roger, sir."

Chapter Twenty-Eight

It was Thomas's wary nature that prompted him to lead Gabriel and Silas into the diner rather than take them straight to the meeting. While his two friends enjoyed a cup of coffee, Thomas's eyes searched the dark shadows for any suspicious movement. Something was bothering him, but he couldn't figure out what it was. Nothing seemed out of the ordinary, but he couldn't shake the feeling that something was not right.

"When shall we go in, Thomas?" Gabriel asked as he finished his coffee.

"Yes," Silas added urgently. "Don't you think we should get to the meeting? We're looking kind of suspicious just sitting here."

"Hmm," Thomas answered as he searched the empty street nervously, "I guess now is as good a time as any. I'll pay, and then we'll leave."

Thomas led them across the street to a seemingly vacant building. Turning to his left, he walked down the dark street beside the brick structure until he came to a wooden door. He knocked once, paused, and then twice more. The door cracked open, and a hand reached out and waved them in.

"I'll wait out here," Thomas whispered and turned to walk cautiously down the dark street.

"Okay, go," Danita said to the officer two minutes after she saw Thomas and his companions leave the diner and head to the meeting. The officer quickly barked orders into his radio, he and his partner jumped out of their car, drew their weapons, and rushed toward the illegal gathering.

Thomas was almost at the end of the building when he thought he heard a radio crackle and feet running. In a panic he spun around and began to sprint back to the side door his friends had entered. He had only taken three strides when he saw a group of police troopers run up to the door, hit it with a battering ram, and push their way in.

"YOU...STOP!" an authoritative voice called from behind. But Thomas did not stop. He continued forward, veering to his left, and leapt onto the top of a dumpster. Without a pause he sprang and grabbed the bottom sill of a second-floor window. Yanking himself up with his powerful arms, his feet landed on the sill and, just as quickly, he jumped to grab the edge of the third-floor window.

"HEY, STOP! STOP!" the officer below screamed, trying to spot a clear target to shoot at in the night shadows. But by this time, Thomas had pulled himself over the edge of the roof.

Thomas was sick to his stomach with regret for allowing Gabriel, Silas, and all the others to get captured. His mind raced to think of something he could do for them, but there was nothing. Thomas wasn't even sure *he* could get down from this building without being caught.

With no other plan, the young agent of God told himself that somehow he had to escape. The only way he could help his friends was to get to Egg and O.G.P. and try to come up with a plan. Thomas looked toward the far end of the block and saw that the building he was on connected with several other buildings all the way to the next street.

Lord, what do I need to know and what do I need to do? Thomas prayed quickly. Almost immediately he thought, *Okay, what I need to know is that the police are aware that I'm up here, so they will be showing up real soon to get me. What I need to do is be someplace other than here as quickly as possible.*

Thomas sprinted as fast as he could across the roofs toward the building on the far end of the block. When he reached the edge of the roof of the last building, he looked over and saw a streetlamp on a pole about ten feet from the corner of the building on which he stood. Apparently he had been spotted, because he also saw several police officers running down the street toward him.

There was no time to think. Thomas took three steps back, raced forward, locked his eyes on the lamp post, and launched himself off the top of the building. He hit the arm of the lamp hard, smacking his chin on the metal, but he managed to hang on. The arm bent under his weight but didn't break off. Quickly dropping to the ground, he raced down the street with three officers a little less than a half a block behind, firing their handguns at him.

Danita felt guilty when she heard the shots and then saw all the prisoners being led out of the building. As she watched them being shoved into the waiting police vans, she had to admit to herself that she felt a little relieved when she didn't see Thomas in the group. Be that as it may, she didn't look forward to having to explain to Trask that the person she had been following, whom she had held up the raid for, had gotten away.

Two hours later Thomas sat in Egg's apartment with his shirt off as O.G.P finished wrapping a bandage around his chest.

"By the grace of God the bullet only creased your chest," O.G.P. announced. "The rib is bruised but not broken. You never did tell us how you got that bad scrape on your chin."

"Does it hurt much?" Egg asked with concern.

"What difference does it make?!" Thomas shot back angrily. "I lost Gabriel and Silas!"

"It wasn't your fault," Egg quickly answered. "The raid wasn't posted on the Security Administration computer until the last minute. I couldn't reach O.G.P., but I was able to contact G.C. and get her to try to intercept you. But by the time she got close, the police were all over the building, and she had to leave to avoid getting caught herself."

"So where do we stand, Egg?" Thomas asked as he painfully pulled his shirt back on.

190

"Well, it's really bad, and it may get a lot worse if we can't come up with something. Gabriel is a very important spiritual leader. It will be hard on all the Christians if we lose him!

"The only thing keeping this from being a total disaster is that, for now at least, the police apparently don't know they've caught Gabriel. The police know about his work and have been trying to catch him for years. From what I have been hearing on the radio, the arresting officers think that Gabriel and Silas are just two of the local ministers whom they haven't yet identified. But when they figure out who they've got, they will torture the two of them until they kill them or get all the information they know…which is a lot."

"What are we going to do?" Thomas asked urgently. "You both know for a fact that the police will eventually discover his true identity."

"Well, first we're going to pray," O.G.P. returned. "Then, when the Lord gives us His answer, we will use all of our brains and resources to get Gabriel and the others out."

"We need more information as quickly as we can get it," Egg announced. "You two start praying, and I will contact our people and get them collecting all that we need to know. Armed with that knowledge, God's direction should make more sense to us. I will be spending most of the rest of the evening searching through the police computer's database, but some information that I need can only be collected by observing what's going on inside the building and talking with some of the employees. I will get G.C. on that. She will be instructed to bring the information I need to you at the coffee shop. She won't get off work until five. Can you meet her there about five-thirty tomorrow afternoon?"

"I think so," Thomas answered thoughtfully. "I'm required to go to a special meeting at the New Self Church tomorrow at two. There'll be a discussion class to follow, but unless I fall asleep in the class and have to stay late, I should be able to make it."

"Then don't fall asleep!" O.G.P. ordered sternly. "Getting this information is a matter of life or death!"

When Thomas saw the serious look on both of their faces, he said to himself, *probably not a good time to say something cute.* He gave them an annoying smile and saluted.

"Now, Thomas, while Egg does his work," O.G.P. announced, "You and I are going to ask God for a miracle."

Chapter Twenty-Nine

After praying with O.G.P., Thomas exited Egg's apartment through the back window and descended the rear corner of the structure until he reached the alley. He hurried up to the street and quickly blended into the crowd of people walking to their destinations. His concerns for Gabriel and Silas weighed heavily on him as he trudged back to his apartment building.

When Thomas finally arrived at his door, he realized that he was pressed for time. He had to push himself to get all of his duties taken care of for his handyman job in order to make it — barely in time — to the church building for his required meeting.

One of the obnoxious young ushers wearing a maroon staff shirt with a button-down collar glared at Thomas as he slipped into the back of the auditorium at the last minute. Thomas responded to the glare with one of his signature annoying smiles. He lifted his arm so that the usher could see the watch he was wearing and tapped it to indicate that, technically, he was on time...barely. "Legalist!" Thomas growled under his breath still smiling.

The first part of the meeting was to be a lecture on good citizenship by an assistant to the Director of Civil Compliance.

Boy, this is gonna be a yawner, Thomas said to himself as he took a deep breath and slid back in his seat while the speaker was being introduced.

The church's executive leader went on and on, praising the accomplishments and honors of their guest speaker. *Great granny's galoshes!* an annoyed Thomas huffed to himself as the introduction seemed to have no end. *Who cares about all this stuff? Just get on with it!*

The speaker continued for several more minutes, and Thomas was ready to pull his hair out when suddenly the gentleman brought his speech to a close. "Ladies and gentlemen, please welcome our very special guest, Ms. Veronica Pearl!"

Thomas joined the others in the auditorium giving the speaker the expected applause and was just settling in to endure the next hour's talk when he suddenly bolted upright in his seat. He was shocked as he stared in amazement at the person now standing behind the podium. *IT'S...IT'S HER!* He thought as he leaned forward with wide eyes. *IT'S REALLY HER! IT'S O.G.P.!*

What did the leader guy say her name was...Veronica Pearl? So O.G.P. is Veronica Pearl! Suddenly a thought came to him, causing him to gasp and almost laugh out loud. *Oh, wow! Now I get it...O.G.P....She's the Pearl Of Great Price like in Jesus's parable!*[14] *That's cute.*

---

[14] Matthew 13: 45-46

Thomas actually heard very little of O.G.P.'s speech. He was too busy trying to understand this powerful woman of God who daily risked her life in Satan's camp doing all she could to serve her King.

What a woman! Thomas thought admiringly. *She has sacrificed everything for Jesus: her family's fortune, a comfortable life, her successful position in the government. And for what? If she's caught, she loses everything and goes to jail, torture, and death — all because of her faith in Jesus Christ. Is Jesus really worth all this?*

Thomas let his mind drift back to his own faithful parents and his life before coming to Christ. He thought back on hiding in the basement apartment when the police were determined to catch him, then eventually coming to his own faith in Jesus. He thought of his baptism in the bathtub of a family he didn't even know and all the ones who had risked their lives to save him and give him a chance to know Jesus. He thought of how unworthy he was to receive the grace of God, and yet God loved him enough to give it to him anyway. He remembered the sense of peace and security he felt when he gave Christ his life. He thought of the new life Christ had given him and his new friends and new family whom he loved as much as his own parents.

All this and heaven too, Thomas concluded his thoughts. *Absolutely…Jesus is worth all this and much, much more!*

When the talk was over, Thomas went to one of the many classrooms and had to endure another hour of indoctrination into the religion of submissive citizenship. He had to work at it, but to his credit,

Thomas managed to keep himself awake and was able to make it to The Cup O' Joy on time.

When he got there, he saw Grace had already arrived and was picking up her hot drink. Thomas quickly went to the counter and ordered one himself. Paying for it and hurrying to the prep station, he set his cup on the station counter beside Grace's drink.

"I hope you didn't order green tea this time," she whispered without looking at Thomas.

"Black coffee," he whispered back with a smile.

"Aww...you remembered." Grace picked up Thomas's cup and walked to a table, taking a seat facing the front door.

Thomas took Grace's cup and let his finger slip underneath. He could feel a folded piece of paper stuck to the bottom which would be the information that Egg needed. He removed the lid to fix his drink and snorted in disgust, "Coffee!"

Snatching up the cup, he walked over to a table beside Grace and sat in the nearest seat with his back to her.

"The last time we met, it was to run one of your secret missions," he heard her whisper. "There was so much happening that we never officially introduced ourselves. I'm G.C."

"They call me Forty-five," he answered, "but that's just my secret agent name. My real name's Twenty-two."

Grace snorted when she heard that and almost spit her sip of coffee onto the table. "So should I call you Twenty, or should we keep it business-like, and I call you Mr. Two?"

"Oooh," Thomas whispered excitedly. "Mr. Two! I like that! It sounds so…so sinister!"

"Sorry I screamed at you in the park the other day, Thomas," Grace said sincerely.

"I under…Hey, wait!" Thomas caught himself. "How did you know my name was Thomas?"

"Maddie, the girl at the counter, and I had a long talk when she and I went to the store to buy all the groceries you wanted to give to the needy family," Grace returned. "Besides, she's a friend of mine, and she tells me all I want to know."

"So you've got your own spy?!"

"Well, a girl has to be careful, you know," Grace shot back. "Besides, I was curious about you."

"I want a spy," Thomas whined.

"You'll just have to get your information the old-fashioned way," Grace returned with a giggle.

"I really would like to ask you out," Thomas returned, "you know, for informational purposes and all. But with our situation like it is, what we're doing now is as close to a date as we're going to have."

"At least for the foreseeable future," Grace added.

Whoa! Thomas thought to himself excitedly when he heard Grace's response, *This is awesome! She didn't shoot me down! Maybe there's hope…after the foreseeable future!*

Just then the bell over the door chimed as someone walked in. Thomas heard Grace whisper, "Uh oh! Gotta go!"

"No, wait!" Thomas hissed back as he heard Grace scoot back her chair and head for the door.

"Well, look who I ran into at my favorite coffee house?" a friendly voice called. After Thomas saw

Grace dash out of the door, he looked for the speaker. With a disappointing sigh, Thomas realized that the person who had just come in was Linda Winters, the young woman he had saved from the police and who he had been trying to avoid for the last several days.

Chapter Thirty

"Coffee, please!" Danita called toward the counter. "And can you bring it to me here?" Without waiting for an answer, she sat down across from Thomas.

"You left the other day before we could plan our next meeting," she began with a smile.

"So I guess this must be it," the young man returned. "You didn't bring your...uh...book this time, did you?"

"No, I've learned my lesson. Thanks so much for all your help. I really got myself in trouble. If it hadn't been for you, I would probably be in jail right now."

"You're welcome," Thomas said.

"How's your week been?" the young woman asked probingly as she studied his face.

"I've had better," Thomas answered. He took a sip of his drink and immediately gagged and almost spilled his cup when he tasted the coffee.

"So are you ready to trust me with your last name?" Linda asked shrewdly.

"I'm just Thomas."

Linda gave him a disappointed look and an annoyed sigh. "Well, Thomas, I'm glad I ran into you again. You have probably guessed that I'm a Christian. And the fact that you helped me get away from the police rather than turning me in tells me that either you're one too, or you're at least sympathetic."

Thomas gave no answer.

"Because I'm new here in town, I'm desperate to find some people who would appreciate that book I was carrying, if you know what I mean. Can you help me?"

"Linda," Thomas began again, "first of all, you've got to be more careful. The police have spies all over the place. I could be one for all you know."

"Because you helped me get away from the police proves that you're not a spy," she countered.

"Unless I helped you in order to win your confidence so you would tell me about other believers you might know."

"Oh," the girl said with surprise, "I hadn't thought of that."

"You could be a spy trying to trap me, for that matter," Thomas returned. "You can't expect people to introduce you to Christians if they don't know you."

"Wow! Finding Christian friends is going to be more difficult than I thought," she said her thoughts out loud, always keeping her eyes on Thomas. "But I did find you. I really need you to be my friend, Thomas. Can we talk sometimes? It gets really lonely when I don't have anyone to talk to."

Thomas thought on the girl's words for a moment and said, "Yeah, we can talk. You said you like to carry the Bible with you."

"It was my mother's," Linda returned.

"Do you read it?" Thomas probed.

"Uh...yeah, yeah, I read it."

"What are you reading in it right now?" Thomas cross-examined.

She was caught off guard by the blunt question. "I'm...uh...reading the part about...uh...Jesus."

"What book of the Bible are you reading in?" Thomas asked again.

"I...uh...don't know," she admitted. "I just, sort of, flip it open and start reading."

"Find the book of John in your Bible and read that," Thomas directed.

"The book of John?"

"Yeah, it's in the back part of your Bible."

"That sounds like you know a lot about it," Linda said with a sly look.

"Well, from what you've said, I may know a little more than you do," Thomas answered. "I'm not saying that I'm a Christian, but if you're serious, here's what I'll do: you read the book of John — the whole book — then we can meet again, and you can tell me what you think about it...and I promise I won't turn you into the police."

"But you do know some Christians you can introduce me to, right?" the woman probed again.

Thomas picked up his cup and stood up without answering her question. "When you finish John, we'll talk again."

"But how will I contact you?" she asked.

"You found me this time. You should be able to find me again."

Turning quickly, Thomas walked out the door.

The young woman kept sipping her coffee but watched the direction Thomas walked. Hurrying to the counter, she paid for her drink and stepped out of the door to follow. Not seeing him, she realized he must have stepped into the alley beside the coffee shop. Rushing to the corner, she peeked into the alley and was stunned to find it empty. Once again, she stomped her foot in anger. *How does he do that?* she growled to herself, then turned to head to Trask's office.

An hour later Thomas stood in Egg's computer room watching the genius study the note Grace had given him. Thomas rocked back and forth impatiently, eager for some information.

"So...what do all those letters and numbers tell you?" Thomas finally blurted out.

"You obviously looked at the note," Egg observed. "Could you make any sense of it?"

"No, not at all!"

Egg smiled at the response. "That's good!" Egg answered. "You weren't supposed to. It's a code that G.C. and I came up with. It's actually easy to read if you know how to do it. What the note tells me is that G.C. was able to find Gabriel in the jail and confirm that he and Silas are there. Right now they and the other believers are being held for questioning, but all of them will be transferred to a more secure prison in a few days."

"Where will they take them?" Thomas asked with concern.

"G.C.'s note says that they are to be taken to Holding Facility 526," Egg paused for a moment as he rapidly typed something on his computer, "which is just outside of Dandenburg."

Egg studied the information on his screen and relayed what he read. "It's a horrible place, Forty-five. We have no record of anyone being released from there…alive."

"Where is this terrible place?" Thomas asked anxiously.

"It's not far. Only thirty miles away."

"You can bet there will be a lot of guards there," Thomas said thoughtfully, "and that means a lot of guns. You aren't planning for us to shoot our way in, are you?"

Egg stopped studying the note and turned to face Thomas. "Forty-five, I know you haven't been a believer for that long, but I hope you know by now that, as followers of Jesus, we don't 'shoot our way in'…or out. We face the problem, see what God has given us, and pray for His solutions. The answers God sends sometimes require that we show creativity, imagination, and occasionally a wee bit of subterfuge, but we won't be killing anyone."

"Okay, got it!" Thomas returned with a salute. "Is there anything I can do to help?"

"While O.G.P. and I gather all of the necessary information, it would help a lot if you pray."

"I'm already doing that, but I guess I can pray more."

"Be sure and check in with me tomorrow," Egg said. "I want to keep you on top of what we are planning because when we decide to make a move, it will have to be done quickly. Do you understand?"

With a nod Thomas headed for the back window to make his exit.

"Wait a minute!" he heard Egg call.

Thomas turned and walked back to his friend.

"Your father's name is James Morrison, right?" Egg asked.

"Right," Thomas returned eagerly. "James Michael Morrison. Have you heard any news about my parents?"

"Not about your mother," Egg returned sadly. "I'm sorry, Forty-five, but I received a report today that James M. Morrison of New Harbor is listed as 'died while incarcerated.'"

The news so shocked him that Thomas stumbled backwards and collapsed into a chair. "Are...are you sure?" he choked out as his eyes filled with tears.

"My source is very reliable," Egg answered. "I'm so sorry!"

For several long moments the grief-stricken young man sobbed with his head in his hands. Egg rolled his wheelchair over and put his hand on his friend's knee.

Finally Thomas looked at Egg and asked, "Did you get any word about my mother?"

"No. I assume she's alive and still in prison."

Dropping his head in his hands, Thomas wept more.

Chapter Thirty-One

The following Sunday, after the church meeting, a somber Thomas kept his eyes open for his new acquaintance, Linda, but didn't see her in the crowd. When the classes and the required assembly dismissed, he left feeling relieved that she hadn't shown up. As he descended the steps of the large, stone building, he was surprised to see her sitting on the rock wall beside the steps, apparently waiting for him.

"Hey," she said, somewhat subdued.

"Hello," Thomas returned as he looked around for eavesdroppers. "Well, did you finish the book of John?" Thomas asked in a low voice.

A brief smile and a nod of her head indicated that she had, but Thomas was concerned when he saw her face. There was a fading bruise on her right cheek that she had tried to hide with makeup, and her over-the-top friendliness was no longer present.

"What's wrong, Linda?" Thomas asked with concern. "What happened?"

"Nothing," she answered, suddenly all smiles and cheerfulness.

"Did someone hit you?"

"Oh, that. I was just clumsy and ran into a door," she said, trying to brush off the question, but Thomas saw tears forming in her eyes.

"No," Thomas persisted. "Something happened to you. What was it?"

At this point Linda let the tears flow. "Can we go someplace to talk?" she asked. "How about the coffee shop where we met before?"

"They're closed on Sundays," Thomas returned. "We could go to the park a couple of blocks over."

"Okay," she sniffed, "let's go there."

"The police picked me up yesterday for questioning," Linda admitted as they walked.

"Yeah," Thomas snarled, his anger starting to rise, "I can see the evidence of their 'questioning' on your cheek. What did they want to know, and what did you tell them?"

The young woman dropped her eyes as she answered. "Oh, I didn't tell them anything about you. They said they had seen my Bible and wanted to know where I got it."

"What'd you say?"

"I played dumb. I said that it was a gift from my grandmother before she died, and I carried it with me in memory of her."

"Did they ask you if you were a Christian?" Thomas probed.

"Uh…They…uh…Well, yes, they did."

"What did you tell them?"

"I…uh…I fooled them," Linda returned with a grin. "I told them that I thought my grandmother had been, but when she tried to talk to me about the Bible, I just thought they were a bunch of crazy stories that didn't make sense. It...uh...took a couple of slaps in the face, but they acted like they believed me and let me go."

Thomas thought on this for a moment and said, "Are you okay?"

"No, Thomas. I'm not!" the woman shot back. "I'm terrified! They know my name. They know where I live. I'm scared to go back to my apartment! Do you know of anyone who can help me? I'm desperate!" As she said this, Linda stopped, threw her arms around the stunned young man, and began to sob on his shoulder.

Thomas was taken aback by the young woman's emotional release. He reached up and reluctantly patted her on the back as she wept. He searched the area where they stood and spotted a black SUV parked a block away.

The young man pulled her away from his shoulder and said, "Listen, it isn't safe here. Come with me. We need to keep moving."

Thomas led the way quickly through the park and out the other side, constantly glancing around them as they walked. Taking the first corner, he hurried them down the street, turning into a narrow alley between two buildings. Coming out the other side, Thomas changed directions and quickly traveled two more blocks. Searching the area, he saw nothing suspicious.

He stopped in front of a multistory building that had a set of steps leading down to a basement apartment. He sat Linda partway down the steps so that she could not be seen from a passing car and said, "I need you to stay here for a few minutes. I think I can help you, but I have to check something out first. Just stay here, and I'll be back for you soon."

Without waiting for an answer, Thomas sprinted off. He ran the remaining five blocks to his apartment building and raced up the stairs all the way to the roof and his laser transmitter. He needed to talk to Egg.

It was almost an hour later when Thomas returned to Linda.

"I thought you had forgotten me!" she snapped irritably.

"Sorry, I had to fold my laundry," he teased.

"So are your friends going to help me?" she shot back, brushing off his joke.

"*I'm* going to help you," he returned evasively. "Here, put these on." Thomas handed her a large dark hoodie and a pair of dark sweatpants. "The pants are mine, so they're big enough for you to pull on without having to take your shoes off."

"What is this for?" she said, a little annoyed.

"I'm taking you to a safe house for now, but it's over ten blocks away, and I don't want you to be recognized."

"You think the police are following me?" Linda asked.

"I guarantee it, so hurry up, and let's get going. And keep your hoodie up."

It took some time to reach the safe house because Thomas took a very round-about way to make sure they weren't being followed.

"So you said you read the book of John?" Thomas asked as they walked.

Chapter Thirty-One

"Yes, I did," the young woman returned.

"Hmmm," he said thoughtfully. "What did you think about it?"

"Well, the first part was kind of confusing. It started talking about *the Word* and that *the Word was with God and was God*.[15] I didn't know what he was talking about until John explained that the Word was Jesus. Why did he call Him *the Word*?"

"John wrote his book to Greeks, and the Eternal Word was a concept they were familiar with," Thomas returned. "But I really think the main reason he did it was to emphasize that Jesus is the perfect expression of God. Later on, Jesus says that He only spoke what He heard from God.[16] At one point He tells the disciples that if they have seen Him, then they have seen the Father in Heaven."[17]

"I remember that," Linda said eagerly. "That's crazy! Really that whole book is crazy. It's just telling you everyday stories about Jesus, and then out of the blue, it talks about Him doing miracles. John describes Jesus healing blind and deaf people, lame people, all kinds of sick people, and even raising people from the dead, but he does it in this mater-of-fact way like it was just everyday stuff!"

"I think it was everyday stuff with Jesus," Thomas returned.

"All right," Linda confronted her companion, "tell me straight. Do you think all of that stuff is real?"

---

[15] John 1: 1
[16] John 12: 49-50
[17] John 14:9

209

"Why are you asking me? You're the one who said you were a Christian."

"Oh…right…about that," she explained, "I said I was a Christian because my grandmother said that years ago she and her family went to a church, and she read her Bible a lot. So that means our family is Christian, right?"

"No, it doesn't, and that's why I don't like using the term," Thomas answered. "It means too many things to too many people. I think using the phrase *a follower of Jesus* is better. So, Linda, are you a follower of Jesus?"

"Since I don't know what that means, then I guess not."

"Being a follower of Jesus means that, when Jesus says that He is King and Lord, you not only accept that to be true, but you believe it strongly enough to commit to letting Jesus be King and Lord over all of your life…ALL of your life. You don't live for yourself anymore, but rather you live your life for Him, making choices and decisions for your life based on what pleases Him."

"WOW!" the young woman exclaimed. "That's a huge commitment! Why would anyone do that, especially for a guy who's been dead for over two thousand years?"

"You read the book!" Thomas returned. "Sure, Jesus died on the cross to pay for all of our sins, but He didn't stay dead. He's alive!"

"You really believe that?" she asked.

"True followers of Jesus do! And they willingly and eagerly make Jesus their Lord and King because what Jesus promises to His followers is a life that is infinitely better than the life you would have without Him as Lord...AND the life He gives goes on forever!

"Okay, this is the place where the safe house is."

They stood in front of a dilapidated, multistory brick building in the middle of a block of other old, rundown buildings.

"I'm not impressed," Linda returned with a disappointed tone.

"You aren't supposed to be," Thomas shot back. "A safe house is not something you want to call attention to. Come on. We need to walk around back."

They traveled to the end of the block, turned the corner, and walked to an alley between the buildings. Moving cautiously until they reached the rear of the derelict structure, Thomas pulled out a key, unlocked a rusty steel door, and led the way in.

It was dark with a slightly musty smell, but when Thomas flipped on a light, Linda was surprised at how clean it was.

"It hasn't been used for a week or so, but it should be clean," Thomas said. After the young woman was inside, he closed the door, flipped a deadbolt lock, and led them down a hallway. The first room they passed was on the right, and from the quick glance Linda got, it seemed to be an office of some type.

"This next door is where you will stay. There aren't any windows, but it does have a bed and a bathroom. There's a staircase at the end of the hall that goes up into the building, but it would be best for you not to go up there. If anyone outside notices a light or sees someone moving inside an abandoned building, they'll just call the police.

"There's some peanut butter and crackers on the shelf over there, and I'll try to bring you some real food tomorrow."

"So how long do I have to stay here?" the woman asked.

"Just a few days probably. I'll need to contact some people and find a safe place for you long term."

Chapter Thirty-Two

Danita, or Linda, as she had identified herself to Thomas, had eaten all of the crackers and half of the peanut butter by the next afternoon. She was licking on a spoonful of straight peanut butter when she heard the door creak at the end of the hallway. Peeking out of the door, she saw Thomas setting the deadbolt behind him.

"You sure take your own sweet time about things," Linda said with an edge of annoyance.

"Sorry," Thomas returned, picking up a large bag of groceries and hurrying to join her. "There's been a lot going on, but I did manage to get you some food."

Linda snatched the bag and rushed to examine its contents.

"So what's happening?" she asked offhandedly when Thomas had joined her.

"I needed to help some friends with a project," Thomas returned evasively. "It's personal, but I should be able to get you to a safe place in another day or so.

"These friends of yours, are they Christians?" Linda asked eagerly. "I would love to meet them! Christians are about the only people I feel I can trust."

"Just be patient," Thomas returned. "Your ordeal should come to an end soon."

Three knocks were suddenly heard at the steel door. These were followed by two more.

"Who's that?" Linda asked with concern.

"It's a friend," Thomas answered. "I'm expecting someone."

Placing his hands on the woman's shoulders, Thomas looked her in the eyes. "Now, Linda," he began seriously, "this is nothing you need to know about. It could even be dangerous to you. So I need you to stay right here in your room while I'm talking with my friend. Will you do that for me?"

"Uh...sure, Thomas. I'll just sit here and fix me something to eat. You go see your friend."

Thomas thanked her and left, closing her door behind him.

Linda noisily removed several of the items in the bag onto the table. Then, kicking her shoes off, she tiptoed to the door and quietly opened it. Stealing a glance down the hallway, she saw that, when Thomas opened the door, a hooded figure in a dark, baggy sweat suit rushed in, and both of them quickly darted into the office room.

Carefully, so as to make no sound, Linda left her room and hurried to the office. Pressing her ear against the door, she could make out their words.

"It's tonight," the stranger said. "The police will be transporting our people from the jail to the prison at Dandenburg. They are to leave the jail at six this evening in some of the vans--with an escort, we expect."

"Multiple vans and police escorts," Thomas repeated. "That's going to make it difficult to get everybody out."

"It doesn't matter!" the stranger shot back. "It has to be done, and we have to succeed! That's why we're using our entire team."

"All of them?" Thomas asked with surprise.

"All of them," came the determined answer.

"So what's the plan?" Thomas wanted to know.

"We will take them at the gate of the prison in Dandenburg. That way they will think they are safe, and their guard will be down. Your job is to coordinate the ambush. It will come from the woods on either side of the main gate. As soon as the police motorcade stops, you are to give the signal, and all of our troopers hiding in the woods will start their attack. While the police are keeping their heads down, I will send in the team to open the vans and release the prisoners. As soon as we free them and get away, give a second signal to let the attackers know to stop and run."

"Well, it sounds simple enough," Thomas said, "but there are a lot of things that could go wrong."

"It's not the best plan in the world, but it is the only one we've been able to come up with on such short notice," the stranger answered. "We didn't find out about the transfer until this afternoon, so we must move quickly to get everyone in position. You know what you need to do, so do it! Remember, the police vans are scheduled to leave the jail at six, so you have to have your people in position at the prison in Dandenburg no later than six fifteen to give yourself time to be ready."

"Man, that's not much time!" Thomas said with concern.

"That means you have to hurry," the stranger shot back, "and I have to go."

Hearing this, Linda rushed quickly back to her room. She had just crossed the threshold when she heard the office door open. After closing the door to her room, she sat down quickly and began to chew on a carrot. Immediately there was a knock, and Thomas entered.

"Hey, you finding something to eat?" Thomas asked with a smile.

Linda nodded as she chewed.

"Listen, I'm sorry, but I've got to go."

"I was hoping you could stay and eat a bite with me," the woman returned with a smile. "Is it something pressing?"

"Yeah, you might say that," Thomas answered. "I'll try to check on you tomorrow. I should have some news for you about where you're going. See you then." Without waiting for a response, Thomas hurried out the door.

Linda waited a moment until she heard the steel door shut and lock, then she stole another peek down the hallway. Rushing back to the chair, she quickly pulled on her shoes and ran to the exit. Flipping the deadbolt, she cracked open the door and studied the alleyway. Convinced that no one was there, she stepped out, pulled the door closed behind her, and raced to the police building.

"What are you talking about?" Trask snapped at her. "We aren't moving prisoners this evening!"

"Well, they think you are," Danita shot back confidently. "They're rushing around right now to put their big ambush plan in place. I heard them say that they are using all of their people to be ready to attack your vans at the gate of the prison in Dandenburg this evening."

"They're using ALL of their people?" Trask asked thoughtfully.

"That's what they said," Danita returned. "They're using all of their people for the ambush."

"Hmmm…This may be the perfect time to take out their whole organization with little risk to us," Trask said excitedly as he rubbed his hands together vigorously.

Instantly the Deputy Administrator jumped from behind his desk and threw open his office door. "Bates, Collier, Drischol, get the S.W.A.T. team and everybody else who can carry a gun! We're leaving for a special mission in twenty minutes!"

"Everybody, sir?" Bates asked in confusion.

"Leave whoever's on duty at the front desk and at the door to the jail. The rest need to be ready to go. We're taking the two prisoner vans without windows, so if anyone's watching, they can't tell that they are filled with officers. NOW MOVE!"

Turning back to the girl, Trask smiled and said, "See, Ms. Jefferson, even you can be helpful with a little motivation."

"I've done my part, Mr. Trask," Danita said angrily. "Now leave me and my family alone!"

"Oh, Ms. Jefferson," Trask returned as he checked to see that his pistol was fully loaded, "you are so short-sighted. I, on the other hand, can see this as the beginning of a very long and productive relationship between us.

"Come in tomorrow morning," he commanded sharply, suddenly changing his tone, "and I'll have your next assignment ready."

Chapter Thirty-Three

Danita remained seated in the chair in front of Trask's desk, seething in anger even after the Deputy Director had left. She was completely disgusted with him. Why had she ever trusted Trask to keep his word? He was a devious, conniving snake who only wanted power and position, and he didn't care who he crushed to get it. As soon as she was of no more use to him, that self-serving slime ball would throw her and her family away like garbage. She was not only furious at Trask, she was mad at herself as well. She felt like a rat.

"What have I done?!" she said out loud. "I betrayed Thomas and his friends just to save me! Thomas isn't a criminal! He's not! He and his friends are only trying to help people. He put himself at risk several times for me, and I turned him in! I turned them ALL in, just like that guy in the book of John I read about. What was his name? Judas! That's me...Danita Judas Jefferson!" As she said this, she buried her head in hands and sobbed.

A moment later Danita's head suddenly jerked up. "No, no, NO!" she exclaimed angrily as she wiped her eyes furiously with the back of her hand. "I WON'T DO

IT!" she exclaimed in rage. "I will NOT be that man's Judas...not if I can help it!"

Jumping out of the chair and hurrying behind the desk, she threw open the shallow wall cabinet she had seen Trask open to collect the van keys he needed. Of the remaining keys hanging there, she grabbed a set, hoping that they belonged to something she could drive, and following the signs on the walls, raced through the empty corridors and down the stairs to the garage.

She was still seething with anger as she burst through the door and ran to the center of the large, cavernous structure. Holding up the keys, she pushed the lock button on the fob. The horn honked and the lights flashed on a black SUV across from her. She raced to the vehicle, unlocked it, and jumped in. Less than a minute later, she was weaving through the streets of Grantham, headed for the highway leading to the nearby town that was her destination.

Once outside of the city, Danita pushed the accelerator to the floor. Just as she reached the outskirts of Dandenburg, she spotted the two vans and an SUV just ahead of her, turning onto an unmarked road that she assumed led to the holding facility. Keeping her distance, she followed the small caravan down the lonely two-lane road through a thick grove of trees.

She saw the vans and car disappear around a curve in front of her, and she slowed her pursuit. As her vehicle eased around the curve, Danita saw the prison in the distance, standing in the center of a clearing in the woods. She parked the SUV in the middle of the road and sprinted through the forest to her right, searching frantically for Thomas and his friends.

She had run through the trees for nearly four minutes when, just ahead of her, she heard what sounded like a gunshot. Suddenly there were twenty or thirty more.

At the sound of the first shots coming from the woods, Trask gave the order. Men in helmets and bulletproof vests, carrying assault rifles, poured out of the police vehicles. The highly trained men spread out, facing both sides of the road, and began to fire rapidly into the dark woods as they advanced. Several armed guards from the prison rushed out of the gates and joined them.

Although Danita couldn't see them, she could hear yelling coming from the direction of the police vehicles as Trask, the S.W.A.T. team, and the others returned fire. Bullets ripped through the branches and trees all around her, but she kept running, yelling for Thomas as she ran.

Suddenly Danita saw a hooded figure racing through the woods ahead of her, running away from the prison and the police.

"THOMAS!" she cried, and the person stopped and turned to face her. "You aren't Thomas!"

The stranger facing her was a woman in her mid-twenties. By the look on her face, she obviously recognized the person who had called her.

"What are YOU doing here?" the stranger asked in surprise.

"I came to warn you!" Danita answered, and then added, "Do you know me?"

"Yes, Ms. Jefferson, I know you, but you shouldn't be here!"

"I know, I know, but this is a trap. The police knew you would ambush them and set a trap to catch all of you. It's my fault that they know, and I had to try to warn you. I couldn't live with myself if I didn't. Where's Thomas?"

"He's not here."

Just then more bullets ripped through the leaves nearby. The stranger reached over and gave Danita a quick hug, saying, "That was brave of you to come all this way to warn us, but we've got to get out of here quickly! How did you get here?"

"After everybody left, I stole a police car and followed them."

"Leave it and come with me!" the woman ordered.

The stranger grabbed Danita's hand and pulled her rapidly through the woods away from the prison as the battle continued behind them. After several minutes of hard running, they sprinted out of the woods onto a logging road where a motorbike was waiting.

Danita bent over with her hands on her knees, breathing hard, as the stranger rushed to the bike. "Get on!" the stranger ordered. "We've got to go!"

"But what about the others?" Danita asked in a panic as she pointed back in the direction of all the continual shooting.

"There are no others."

"What?" Danita asked in surprise. "I don't understand. If there are no others, who started all the shooting?"

"Firecrackers!" the girl grinned back as she kick-started the bike. "I set them up on both sides of the road and lit the fuses when I saw the police approaching."

"Firecrackers! Why?"

"This is a diversion. No offense, Ms. Jefferson, but we knew you were working with the police. I'm not going to explain, but I know you've been meeting with Trask. So we decided to let you listen in on some of our fake plans, knowing that you'd tell the police about them. The real rescue is happening right now back at the jail. With all of the agents and officers out here, the jail has to be almost empty. We just didn't know that you would have a change of heart and put yourself in the middle of our plans. I'm proud of you, by the way."

"I'm so confused!" Danita sighed as she dropped onto the seat in dismay. Finally she asked, "Who are you?"

The stranger turned and smiled at her. "You can call me G.C.," she said as she twisted the accelerator, causing the dirt bike to shoot off like a rocket.

Chapter Thirty-Four

After scaling the back corner of the city Security Administration building, Thomas crept across the roof quickly to the square metal housing covering the building's ventilation shaft. From the backpack supplied by Egg, he pulled out a pair of night vision goggles. Under the greenish glow of the infrared light, he snatched up a small, battery-operated electric screwdriver and began removing the screws that secured the housing cover. Once off, the two-foot square opening of the vertical shaft was revealed.

Thomas pulled out a short cord, attached one end to the loop on top of his pack, and clipped the other end securely to his belt. Pulling on a pair of neoprene gloves, Thomas dropped the pack down the hole ahead of him and, using the gloves and the rubber soles of his shoes, he slowly and carefully slid down the metal duct. He took his time in order to descend as quietly as possible. Eight floors needed to be traversed to reach the basement where the jail was located. He let gravity do most of the work, using the friction of his shoes and gloves to keep him from sliding too quickly.

When he finally reached the main floor, he crept along the horizontal ductwork until he found a vent. Spying through the grates, Thomas spotted the sign-in desk about ten feet to his left. One bored guard sat at the desk playing solitaire on the computer, and another sat a short distance away carelessly watching a set of monitors of the video feeds of the security cameras in the cell block. To the right of Thomas's view was the door leading down a flight of stairs to a locked door into the actual jail. Once he identified how many guards were present, Thomas quietly returned to the vertical descent of the ventilation shaft and carefully slid to the bottom floor. He hurried along the horizontal duct until he came to a turn where the ventilation passage passed through the wall and into the cell block. When he arrived at the first vent, he took a moment to study the room below. Satisfied that no guards were present, he pulled a small, battery-operated disc grinder from his pack and quickly cut through two of the bolts holding the vent cover in place. He bent the flimsy metal cover down, pulled a ski mask over his face, and dropped quietly to the floor.

"Dude, what are you doing?" a voice from one of the cells asked. Thomas put his finger to his lips and removed the cord holding his pack to his belt. Rushing back to the steel door that led to the stairs, Thomas stole a glance through the reinforced window in the door and saw the guards from the floor above come charging down the stairs. They had seen him!

Thomas quickly looped one end of the stout rope around the doorknob; the other end he looped around the bars of the cell directly across from the door. There

226

was a loud thump on the door, followed by the guards yelling at him. He could hear their key frantically being jammed at the lock. Thomas pulled the rope tight and tied it securely, preventing the guards from opening the door.

Leaving the furious guards, Thomas rushed to the back of the cell block until he came to a rusty-looking metal door at the end of a row of cells. Whipping out his disc grinder, he quickly cut through the locking bolt and yanked the door open.

"Glad to see you made it," Thomas said to the five masked agents waiting on the other side.

"Yeah, you too," a voice shot back from the darkness.

"The guards spotted me, so we have to work fast," Thomas called as he and the others ran to the cell doors and began cutting at the lock bolts. As soon as a cell was opened, all the prisoners inside were rushed to the rusty door at the rear of the block. Thomas was relieved to find Gabriel and Silas. He revealed himself to them and assured them that his friends would get them to safety.

Within two minutes all of the prisoners were holding hands and being led through the rusty, dark opening and into the musty boiler room below the jail. Using their night vision goggles, the rescuers directed the freed prisoners to the far end of the room where some steps led down into a five-foot-square drain pit. An iron grate propped to the side revealed an opening in the floor leading into the city storm drains.

Thomas was helping the last few prisoners into pit when he heard loud banging on the main entrance to the cell block and knew the guards would be forcing the door open any moment.

"Are you comin'?" a voice shouted at him from the darkness below as he assisted the last three into the dark sewer opening.

"No!" Thomas shouted back. "Get them out of here! I'll distract the guards!"

"BUT..."

"Don't worry! I'll get out another way!" Thomas shot back. "Now hurry! GO!"

"Just so you know," the voice in the darkness called up, "we're going to spot weld the grate so neither you nor the guards can follow us!"

"Got it!" Thomas yelled his understanding. "I'm going to go give you time to do it!" He then turned and ran to the other end of the cell block.

When Thomas arrived at the main door, he saw that the two guards had found a tire tool and were trying to break the double-layered, reinforced glass in the door. They had busted the glass on their side and cracked the glass on the jail side, but they were having trouble breaking through the wire mesh reinforcing the window.

If they broke a big enough hole in the window, they could stick a hand through and cut the rope. Thomas whipped off his pack and shoved it up against the spot on the window they were trying to break through.

The guard with the tire iron flipped it around and began ramming the wedge end into the exposed wires in the window, snapping them and shattering the remaining glass on the other side. When the guard saw Thomas bracing his backpack against the hole he had just made, he glared angrily at him. Yelling at his opponent, the guard whipped out his service weapon and pointed it straight at Thomas.

Instantly Thomas snatched up his pack and raced back into the cell block as a bullet shattered the glass in the door where he had been standing. When he got to the open vent in the ceiling, he tossed up his pack and jumped with all of his strength. He grabbed the metal edges of the vent opening with his gloved hands and drew himself into the air duct with seemingly little effort.

A moment later the guard cut the rope, jerked open the door, and rushed into the cell block. The one who had fired his handgun stopped under the open vent. He saw no signs of the masked intruder, but he could hear him crawling rapidly through the air ducts above him.

The other guard raced through the jail looking for prisoners. He found the opened service door and rushed in, his weapon in one hand and a flashlight in the other.

"They must have taken them out through the storm drain," the second guard announced when he returned, "but they welded the grate. I can't budge it!"

"Well, we know this guy is still in the building," the first guard said, pointing his weapon at the opening. "The building is locked, so he had to have gotten in from the roof. Boost me up, and I'll keep pushing him. You run to the roof and be waiting on him."

The first guard pulled off his shoes and socks as well as his service belt. Shoving his handgun in his waistband, he announced that he was ready. The second guard strained to lift him up and, with a lot of grunting, managed to push the first guard high enough to grab the vent.

"I've got the edge!" the first guard called. "You push while I pull!"

With great effort and help from the other officer, he managed to pull himself up into the air duct. Looking back down, he said, "It's dark up here. Toss me my flashlight, then radio the boss and tell him what happened. But be quick! I need you to get to the roof as fast as you can! NOW GET GOING!"

By this time Thomas had made it through the ducts and back to the vertical part that led up to the roof. Using his hands and feet, he began climbing the air duct. To give himself more room as he crawled and climbed, he wore his backpack in front.

Thomas was pushing himself to climb as fast as he could when he heard thumping and bumping in the air duct behind him. Suddenly a beam of light shot up from the darkness below, revealing the climber.

"HOLD IT RIGHT THERE!" the officer yelled from the bottom of the metal airway.

Thomas quickly yanked his own rubber-coated flashlight from his pocket and bounced it off the wall, which caused lots of noise as it ricocheted repeatedly toward the officer below.

Hearing the racket and seeing the strange object bouncing towards him, the startled officer threw himself back down the horizontal duct, dropping his own flashlight in the process. The light source switched off when it hit, shrouding everything in darkness. The frustrated officer had to spend several long moments groping around until he found his light and could get it turned back on again.

"I SAID *STOP!*" the officer screamed when he had illuminated his quarry again.

But Thomas didn't stop. He was only a couple of feet from the horizontal ducts servicing the third floor.

"STOP, OR I SHOOT!"

Chapter Thirty-Five

Thomas launched himself for the opening just as three shots were fired from below.

"BOGGS! YOU IDIOT!" a voice screamed from far up the shaft. "STOP SHOOTING! YOU ALMOST HIT ME!"

"SORRY! HE JUST DUCKED INTO A SIDE PASSAGE!" Boggs screamed to his partner.

"WHAT FLOOR?"

"Uh...I'm not sure? Let me count."

"WHAT?"

Boggs used his flashlight to count the side openings above him.

"HE'S ON THE THIRD FLOOR, GIBSON!" Boggs shouted up to his partner. "GET DOWN THERE QUICK!"

"ARE YOU KIDDING ME?" Gibson screamed down. "I JUST ABOUT HAD A HEART ATTACK RUNNING UP HERE TO THE ROOF, AND YOU WANT ME TO RUN DOWN TO THIRD?"

"QUIT GRIPING AND DO IT!" Boggs yelled back, starting the climb to the opening his quarry had taken.

Thomas rushed forward along the small passage until he came to a vent in the floor of the duct. Snatching the disc grinder out of his pack, he quickly set to work on the bolts securing one end of the vent cover. In less than a minute, they were cut, and Thomas stomped hard on the end of the metal cover, bending it down into the hallway below.

Just as a flashlight beam lit up the duct, Thomas dropped through the opening, landing hard on the carpeted floor. Springing to his feet, he raced to the stairwell at the end of the hall.

Officer Gibson was red-faced and gasping for breath as he reached the third-floor landing. He jerked open the door and rushed into the hall. Just then a backpack slammed hard into his shins, causing the exhausted officer to launch forward and slam head-first into the wall, dropping his gun. When he collapsed, he left behind a prominent, head-shaped dent in the sheet rock.

Thomas kicked the gun further down the hallway, leaped over the fallen officer, and raced down the stairwell.

A few seconds later a barefoot Boggs dropped out through the ceiling vent and stumbled over to his prone companion.

"Where is he, Gibson?" the weary officer huffed. "You didn't let him get a way, did you?"

Gibson's pained response was a deep, raspy wheeze.

Thomas leaped down the three flights of stairs and sprinted to the lobby of the building. He was hurrying for the front door when something on the wall caught his eye.

"I know that guy!" Thomas exclaimed as he viewed the photographs of the Security Administration officials hanging there. One picture in particular gripped his attention. It was the second one down — the Deputy Administrator Devlin Trask. Thomas began slowly walking toward the photo as he closely studied the man's face. The jet black hair, the goatee, the sharp chiseled features — it was the same guy!

"YOU!" Thomas spat furiously. "You're the weasel-faced scumbag who arrested my folks, and because of you, my dad is dead!" Without thinking, Thomas snatched up a heavy stapler sitting on the welcome desk and hurled it with all of his strength into the face on the wall. The picture frame exploded into hundreds of tiny shards of glass.

Thomas watched the damaged picture flutter down and land face up on the floor. Stepping deliberately to it, he stomped on the face, grinding his heel into it. "MY PARENTS HAVE BEEN TORTURED, AND MY DAD HAS BEEN KILLED — ALL BECAUSE OF YOU!"

Again he stomped on the picture. "AAAAAH!!" he screamed in uncontrolled rage. "I WILL...FIND...A WAY...TO GET MY HANDS ON YOU, TRASK," Thomas sobbed in blind fury, "AND WHEN I DO, I WILL END YOUR STINKIN' CAREER! AAAAAH!!" The young man spoke these words earnestly as he glared at the face in the picture and shook with rage. "COUNT ON IT!"

Just then he heard noise in the distance behind him. The upset young man quickly exited the building and rushed into the night.

He was four blocks away when he heard a chorus of sirens coming from the east and heading toward the jail.

Oh, I'd love to see that no-good weasel's face when he discovers we've cleaned out his dungeon! Thomas snarled angrily to himself as he turned to the right into an alley and raced to the drainage canal that ran through the city.

When he reached the large, public storm drain, Thomas paused to catch his breath. For the next fifteen minutes he ran north along the bank of the drainage ditch, past buildings and warehouses. He arrived at a parking lot where a paneled truck was parked near the canal. Slipping on his night vision goggles, Thomas was relieved to see his team leading the rescued prisoners out of a drain opening in the side of the canal.

They halted suddenly when they saw Thomas approach.

"Forty-Five, is that you?" a voice called from the dark shadows of the canal.

"It's me!"

"We were worried about you," the voice called back as the line of prisoners began moving again. "Did you have any trouble?"

"No," Thomas returned tersely and began helping guide the rescued captives up the side of the canal and into the back of the truck. They were just getting the last of the prisoners loaded when G.C. came trotting up.

"What are you doing here?" Thomas snapped when he saw his friend arrive.

"Nice to see you too," she teased.

"I have three more rescues," she announced with a smile. Grace turned and pointed back the way she had come. Three figures hurriedly made their way across the parking lot towards them.

When they got close enough, Thomas was stunned to see that one of them was Danita Jefferson.

"GRACE!" Thomas snapped furiously. "WHAT ARE YOU DOING—BRINGING THAT SNAKE HERE? SHE BETRAYED US!"

"It's okay, Thomas," Grace answered surprised at Thomas's anger. "She finally chose a side."

"Thomas, I'm so sorry!" Danita said sincerely as she and the others stepped up to them. "You were right. I was working for the police, but I had to. Trask threatened to throw my parents in prison for the rest of their lives if I didn't. And, yes, I told the police about your plans to raid the prison at Dandenburg, but my conscience bothered me so much that I couldn't let them trap you."

"*Hee, hee.* She stole a police car and followed them out to the prison just to warn you," Grace added. "Can you believe that?"

"Really?" Thomas asked in disbelief. "Why would you do that?"

"Because none of you are criminals!" she answered. "All you're doing is risking your lives to help people whose only crime is believing in Jesus. I couldn't live with myself if I helped Trask catch all of you."

"You realize that you're in big trouble now, right?" Thomas asked.

"I was going to be in trouble regardless," Danita returned. "Trask wasn't going to let me go. I figured that I'd rather be in trouble with him than in trouble with God."

"That's why I brought her here," Grace inserted. "If she's going to risk prison for us, we need to help her."

"Who are these others?" Thomas demanded.

"These are my parents," Danita said, throwing her arms around her family. "When I explained my situation to G.C., she said we all needed to come."

"We have friends who will take you to another city and help you create new identities," Grace said. "They're about ready to leave, so let's get you and your folks loaded in the truck. You've got a long way to go tonight."

"Thank you all so much," Danita said sincerely, looking at Thomas and G.C., "but can I ask a question?"

"What is it?" Thomas answered bluntly.

"I've tried to explain to my parents about the things I've read in the Bible," Danita began, "but we all have a lot of questions. Will someone be riding with us who can answer them?"

Thomas said nothing and looked away. Finally Grace said, "I can go. I would love to tell you about my King."

Grace climbed into the back of the truck, looking with concern at Thomas as he turned and stalked angrily away.

Chapter Thirty-Six

For the next several days, Thomas was completely obsessed by thoughts of Devlin Trask. The more Thomas thought about the pain the evil man had caused him and his family, as well as countless others, the more his anger and rage began to control him.

Sleep was out of the question. Every time he tried to lie on his bed and close his eyes, Trask's face was all he saw. It always ended the same way: with Thomas in red-faced fury, beating up or choking his pillow. He couldn't shake his all-consuming hatred of Trask, but to be honest, he didn't try to. In a very dark part of him, a part of him that hadn't been awakened for a long time, this seething hatred felt good.

He was in the process of cutting a beef stick when he looked down at the knife in his hands. "If I could get my hands on you, Trask," Thomas snarled fiercely as he glared at the weapon, "you would *never, EVER* hurt another person!" Like lightning, he drew back and stabbed the beef stick so wrathfully that the knife went through the meat and embedded in the counter.

At the same moment there was a knock at his apartment door, causing him to whip around like a trapped animal. With the second set of knocks, he heard a voice call to him through the door. "Thomas, open up! It's Mike Schuster!"

The angry young man gave an annoyed growl. He did not want to talk to Mike or anyone else right now.

"Thomas, it's been three days since anyone has seen you! I know something's upsetting you. Please open up, and let's talk about it!"

I don't need to talk! Thomas snarled to himself. *I need to do something about it!*

He paused just long enough to yank the knife out of the counter. As he did so, the beef stick fell to the floor with a loud, squishy smack.

"Thomas, I can hear you! I know you're in there!" Mike called through the door. "Please open up! We're all praying for you!"

Hearing that, Thomas looked at the door sadly for a moment, but only for a moment. He shook his head as if to answer with a violent *NO*, and quickly the overwhelming, soul-possessing anger surged back again. Thinking once more of his parents' suffering, Thomas made his fateful decision. He shoved the knife in his belt and raised the window. Snatching up his backpack, he stepped out onto the rain-soaked ledge even as Mike continued to pound on the door and call imploringly to his friend.

Thomas moved like a cat along the narrow shelf until he reached the decorative, protruding bricks that formed the corner of the building. Ignoring the evening shower, he scaled these like a ladder and quickly reached the roof.

As he stood in the rain, something in the back of his mind was telling him not to do this, but his fierce anger quickly cut it off. *"Don't do this*? ARE YOU KIDDING ME!?"* Thomas snarled at the thought. "That worthless sack of filth has tortured and killed innocent people...good people, like my parents! He deserves no mercy, and he'll get none!"

The rain began to fall in earnest as he took a moment to get his bearings, then Thomas carefully planned his path to his victim's office. With grim determination, Thomas left to bring well-deserved justice to Devlin Trask.

Two hours later, Thomas Westcott stood in the heavy downpour on the roof of the structure just to the north of the Security Administration building. The fact that he was soaked to the skin meant nothing to him.

It had taken some time, but moving from rooftop to rooftop as he circled the government building, the hate-filled young man had finally discovered Trask's office. Using binoculars from the equipment he kept in his backpack, Thomas spied on his unsuspecting enemy.

"There you are, you rat!" the angry young man growled as he watched the Deputy City Administrator. Thomas stood like a wet statue as he studied his victim. Trask was pacing up and down in his office, waving a file and yelling at a small crowd of people.

"Well, somebody's upset," Thomas chuckled deviously to himself. "I wonder if it has anything to do with an empty jail. Go ahead; rant and rave, you slime ball! Get all your last, sadistic joy from bullying those poor people because I'm ending your evil career tonight!"

Thomas knew he couldn't get into the building and make it up to Trask's fifth floor office without being stopped. He could surrender himself. He felt sure Trask would want to interview him personally. That would get him close to Trask, but most likely he would be handcuffed, and they would definitely relieve him of his knife.

"No, I've got to take him outside the office, when he's alone and the arrogant rat doesn't suspect anything," Thomas thought out loud as his white knuckles revealed the tense death grip with which he clutched the binoculars.

It was starting to get dark. He checked his watch and saw that it was almost time for the office staff to leave. Thomas hoped that Trask was a workaholic and that he would stay late. "That would give me an opportunity with him alone in the garage," he said with purpose. "But alone or not, he dies tonight."

For thirty more minutes Thomas stayed on the roof top in the cold rain, staring at his victim through the binoculars. He shivered with chill in the soaking downpour, but he wouldn't move. Finally he saw Trask throw down his files and look at his watch. He furiously wrote some notes on his desk calendar and rose to put on his coat.

Thomas sprang into action. Shoving the binoculars into his pack, he slung it on his back and dropped over the corner of the building. It was too dark for anyone to see him descending the wall, but if they did, they would have thought they were watching a human spider. He climbed carefully down one floor until he reached a fire escape. Dropping lightly onto the platform, he hurried down the steps until he reached the second floor and was able to drop to the ground.

Keeping to the darkening shadows, he rushed across the street and into the opening of the parking garage beneath the security building. When he arrived, the garage was empty of people, and there were only six cars still in their parking spaces.

Thomas wasn't sure which car was Trask's, so he hid behind a thick, concrete support pole near the center of the large area. There was a small, green compact car parked beside the pole. Thomas didn't think that would be Trask's, but it was a good spot to wait since he could reach anywhere in the garage quickly from where he hid.

So intent was he on killing his prey that Thomas hadn't even planned an escape route. *I just need to calmly walk up to him when he comes out and ask him for directions to the police desk,* he thought. *I'll even smile as I approach him. He'll never know anything until the moment I strike with my knife.*

"Come on, you rat!" Thomas raved eagerly as his fingers clenched tightly around the handle of his weapon. "Come get what you deserve!"

Chapter Thirty-Seven

The wait for his victim to appear seemed endless to Thomas. Water from his soaked body and clothing made a puddle around his feet as he waited in the parking garage for his mortal enemy to arrive. Thomas's racing heart pounded inside of his chest, and his breathing was shallow and rapid. At that demon-inspired moment, the only purpose Thomas could see for his life was to kill Devlin Trask, and he was extremely anxious to accomplish the task. After several nerve-wracking minutes, Thomas finally heard the door that led from the building into the garage open. He quickly slipped off his backpack, dropped it beside the car next to him, and seated his fingers more securely on the knife handle.

He pressed against the concrete support pillar as he tensed to spring at his victim. He could hear the steps coming closer, and he readied himself. The person was coming straight for him, and the thought suddenly came to him that this might not be Trask, so he stole a peek around the pole to check.

Suddenly a woman screamed and called nervously, "WHO ARE YOU, AND WHAT ARE YOU DOING BESIDE MY CAR?"

"Oh...uh...sorry, ma'am," Thomas said evasively as he hid his knife behind his back. "I didn't mean to scare you, but I was just...uh...waiting for someone."

"Thomas, is that you?"

On hearing his name, Thomas looked at the woman's face. "G.C.!"

"Thomas, everyone has been worried sick about you! No one has seen you or talked to you in days! I could tell the other night that you were upset, and I wanted to talk with you, but you never showed up at the coffee shop."

Thomas had no answer, so he turned and looked away.

That's when she saw the knife. "What's going on, Thomas?! What are you doing here?!"

When he still didn't respond, Grace grabbed Thomas's arm and spun him around to face her. "You're carrying a knife, Thomas! What are you planning to do?!"

"I'M GOING TO KILL TRASK!"

"No, Thomas!" she gasped. "You can't! Why would you do that?"

"I saw his picture on the wall when I escaped from the jail, and I remembered him, Grace! He was the one who arrested my parents and hit my father. He sent them off to prison to be tortured, and I just found out that my father is dead...all because of HIM!"

"Thomas, I'm so sorry," Grace said tenderly.

"My mother may be dead too for all I know, all because of that worthless snake Trask! But he won't hurt anybody else! I'm seeing to that tonight!"

"You can't do this, Thomas!" Grace pleaded. "This is not why Jesus saved you!"

"Don't you see?" Thomas shot back. "Trask must be stopped!"

"And he will be," Grace returned, "but not by you! Vengeance is God's job, not ours.[18] As soon as we give in to revenge, Satan wins. You're doing exactly what Satan wants you to do because, when you give into revenge, you become exactly like the person you hate. Killing Trask makes you just like him, Thomas!"

"Grace, the man has destroyed my life!"

"Yes, he has destroyed your old life," Grace returned, "but God has given you a brand-new life in Jesus...a life free of hatred and full of peace and love...a life where we can turn over all of our past hurts to Him, knowing that He will carry them for us and take care of all of them in the right way. If you remember, Isaiah prophesied that Jesus *has borne our griefs and carried our sorrows.*[19] He ALREADY has taken them, but you have to let go!"

"The man killed my father!" Thomas snapped back. "MY FATHER! How can a person give something like that to God?"

"I did," Grace answered with a smile.

"What do you mean?"

---

[18] Romans 12: 17-19
[19] Isaiah 53: 4

"Five years ago next month, my father was arrested by the secret police. He and my mother had started several house churches, and he was a preacher and Bible teacher for them. I guess the government decided that he was causing too much trouble, so they dragged him off to prison. Three days after they arrested him, we found his lifeless, broken body lying on the sidewalk in front of our house as a warning to us. My mother never got over it. After grieving for a week, she had a stroke and died the same day."

"Your father AND your mother...you must hate them!" Thomas exclaimed, his anger boiling.

"Oh, I'll admit that I struggled for a while," Grace returned. "But eventually I started listening to God instead of Satan. You know, God's Son was tortured and murdered by wicked people too, so He understands. And what did Jesus say after all the suffering? As He hung there dying on the cross, He said, 'Father, forgive them, for they don't know what they are doing.'[20]

"Thomas, it wouldn't surprise me in the least to find out that both your father and mine said something similar as they faced death for Christ.

"It's the followers of Satan who torture and kill, not the followers of Christ. Don't do this, Thomas! Jesus, your parents, and my parents have paid too high a price for you to give it all up for something as foolish and unsatisfying as vengeance."

---

[20] Luke 23: 34

Tears flowed down Thomas's cheeks as he answered her, "I don't know if I can stop, Grace! I'm hurting so badly, and I'm SO ANGRY!"

"But that's what God's grace is for!" she returned, placing her hand on Thomas's arm. "A few of the things God does with His grace is to give us the ability to want what He wants and the strength and motivation to do the things that we are unable to do ourselves. That's in the Bible...in Philippians chapter two, verses twelve and thirteen. When I discovered those two verses, everything changed in my life. I asked Jesus and God gave me the grace to forgive the people who were responsible for my parents' deaths.

"You see, Thomas, as long as you stay in the place of bitterness and unforgiveness, there is no grace there, and those powerful feelings will destroy you. But if you ask God to carry you past those evil attitudes to the place of forgiveness and peace, there is always enough grace for you to do God's will...always!

"And don't you remember? If you won't forgive others, then God won't forgive you.[21] That's the thing that got to me. It helped me to realize that, by forgiving the people who hurt me, God's forgiveness in my heart rescued me from any further damage they could do to me."

"You're telling me that I'm supposed to just let Trask off the hook for all he's done?!"

"Yes, I am!" Grace shot back earnestly. "But remember, Thomas, you might be letting Trask off *your* hook, but God isn't letting him off *His*.

---

[21] Matthew 6: 14-15

"Please, Thomas, let God handle this! It helped me a lot to understand that God loved my parents more than I did, and He knows the very best way to deal with things like this. He watched evil men torture and kill His Son too.

"Ask Him, Thomas! Ask our Father to give you the grace to forgive this man and to free you from Satan's grip on your heart! He will! I promise you He will!"

Tears flowed down Thomas's cheeks as he gave a deep sigh and prayed, "Lord Jesus, help me!"

The soft weeping suddenly burst into sobs as he slowly held out his hand and gave Grace the knife. She received the weapon with relief and wrapped her arms around the grieving, repentant young man.

"Is everything all right, Grace?" a stern voice called from across the garage.

Looking up, both Grace and Thomas saw Trask staring at them suspiciously with his hand on his hip where his service weapon was holstered. Grace quickly moved the hand holding the knife behind her back.

"Yes, Mr. Trask!" she called back with a smile. "Thank you for checking on me, but this is a dear friend of mine who is meeting me here."

With a nod Trask moved his hand away from his pistol and turned to walk to his car.

"I FORGIVE YOU!" Thomas suddenly called out emotionally.

With wild eyes Grace tried to hush him.

Trask stopped and turned again to face the couple with a look of confusion.

Grace smiled and shrugged her shoulders at her boss.

Chapter Thirty-Seven

"Your friend's kind of strange," Trask finally said.

"Oh, he is that!" Grace called back with a laugh.

"Have...uh...have a nice evening, sir!"

As they watched Trask drive past them and out of the garage, Thomas felt something that he hadn't felt in days...peace. Thomas looked his friend in the eyes and smiled at her. "Thank you!" he said sincerely. "God used you to save me from a horrible mistake."

"Well," she responded with a mischievous smile, "my name *is* Grace."

Chapter Thirty-Eight

Even though he was sopping wet, Grace had Thomas throw his pack into the back of her car, and she drove them both to The Cup O' Joy. It was past closing time for the coffee shop when they arrived. Grace parked nearby, and they both ran through the rain to the side door in the alley. After pounding on the metal door for almost a minute, it swung open, bathing the wet couple in a bright yellow light.

"THOMAS!" cried a distraught voice, and Mike rushed out into the rain to hug his friend. "I was so scared for you!" he exclaimed as tears streamed down his face.

"Can we come in, Mike?" Thomas asked as he patted his friend's shoulder. "I've got a lot to talk to you about."

"Absolutely!" Mike agreed eagerly as he ushered his two friends out of the rain and into his apartment.

"Oh, and by the way," Thomas added sincerely, "thanks for not giving up on me!"

The next evening Thomas was sitting in Egg's apartment, his head down and his hands between his knees. O.G.P. was also there. When she heard that their missing agent was coming in, she was determined to join Egg in finding out what had happened.

Thomas was thoroughly embarrassed and ashamed about all that had transpired, but he was determined to come clean about the whole episode. He had been reminded what it's like to be held in Satan's demonic grip. He wanted to remember the shame and guilt so that he would never give in to unforgiveness and vengeance again.

With a gentle nod from Egg, Thomas began telling his story. Once he started, he took his time explaining everything.

"I can't believe that!" O.G.P. said in shock as Thomas concluded his confession. "You were actually going to kill him?"

"Yes, I was," Thomas answered matter-of-factly. "I didn't think about it being wrong. I was already upset because Egg told me that my father had died in prison. Then, when I recognized Trask's picture as the one who arrested and mistreated them, it was more than I could stand. I finally had a person who I could direct all of my rage at, and I did. In fact, I became so angry at that moment that I let Satan take over that area of my heart. I guess that was all the enemy needed, because he quickly took over the rest of me as well. It was a very powerful experience—one that I don't ever want to have again!"

"Couldn't you stop it?" Egg asked.

"No, I couldn't! But to be honest, I didn't want to." Thomas answered sincerely. "That's what was so scary! Satan's grip on my heart in that instant was so powerful that the hatred felt impossible to fight against, and like I said, while consumed with all those intense emotions, I really didn't want to resist it. I hated Trask so much that I would have killed him without hesitation, or at least I would have tried to."

"Or he may have killed you!" Egg observed.

"You're right. That's entirely possible," Thomas agreed, remembering the service weapon on Trask's hip. "It would have been a disaster either way — if God hadn't put Grace there to stop me."

"She called in last night after she got you back to your apartment to let us know what had happened," Egg returned. "I can't tell you how concerned we were for you! I'll admit that, when Grace told me, I cried. And when I told O.G.P., she did too."

"I know as a follower of Jesus that I'm not supposed to worry," O.G.P. said, "but Egg and I were worried sick about you, and that's a fact! Egg thought it might have something to do with your father being killed, but we never dreamed that you were going after the Deputy Administrator. It still stuns me to realize that you were considering murder!"

"It stuns me too...now," Thomas explained. "When I gave in to the hatred, it just took me over. I really don't have anyone to blame but myself. When I let the anger and hate in, that was all Satan needed. Giving in to sin gave the enemy power. Once my hate invited Satan into my heart, he grabbed me and forced me onto a path that I couldn't get off. Between Satan's deceit and my hatred, I couldn't think straight. The only thing that was in my head was how much I hated Trask for what he had done to my family. It felt like I was literally powerless to stop myself from what I was about to do...until Grace reminded me that, in Christ, God has given me the strength to turn away from Satan, the world, and the pull of sin.

"In desperation I cried out to Jesus. The instant I did that and asked Him to help me, the intensity of the temptation to kill that man began to lessen. It's strange, but at that exact moment I could actually feel the strength of the sinful desire start to fade. Don't get me wrong; it was still there, but it was no longer overwhelming. I suddenly had the power to resist it, and through Grace's repeated encouragement, I did."

"Are you okay now?" Egg asked with concern.

"Yeah, I'm doing fine, but I've agreed to do some counseling with a couple of believers."

"I think that's wise, Forty-five," O.G.P. agreed. "Who will you be counseling with?"

"My buddy Mike Schuster insisted that I have dinner with him and his wife each evening for the next week. We'll be spending that time talking about what happened and trying to work through all this."

"That's good," Egg said with a nod. "Mike and his wife have faced quite a few difficulties and trials, and they can teach you a lot about turning to Jesus in those times, rather than to anger or bitterness. Yeah, Mike is a good one to talk to."

"Yep, he is," Thomas agreed, "and his wife is also a really good cook. Talk about a win/win situation!"

"Who's the other person you'll be counseling with?" O.G.P. probed.

Thomas grinned at her question. "Well, the other one is even more like mixing business with pleasure."

"Oh, no!" O.G.P. gasped as realization began to sink in.

"Yessiree!" Thomas announced with a big grin. "Grace has agreed to spend some quality time with me. I believe she feels that God has called her to help me become the man I'm meant to be," Thomas said proudly.

"Have mercy!" O.G.P. groaned as she put her head in her hands. "That girl may need a chaperone for a counseling session with you!"

"Why, O.G.P.," Thomas replied with a mischievous smile, "I'm surprised at you! Remember it's *me* she'll be counseling with."

"My mistake," O.G.P. shot back. "TWO chaperones!"

"Forty-five, do you think that's a good idea?" Egg asked cautiously. "It could be dangerous if you and G.C. are seen together."

"Nothing to worry about, Egg ol' buddy," Thomas returned with the same big grin. "I'm way ahead of you on the whole risk-avoidance thing. Brilliant minds have pondered that worrisome dilemma, and I can say with complete assurance, the potential problem has been solved. Thanks to you, Grace and I will conduct our counselling session, slash date, with the utmost subterfuge and caution."

Thomas Westcott: God's Shadow Agent

Chapter Thirty-Nine

Later that day, right at noon, Thomas sat on a park bench near the entrance of the Security Administration building. Beside him was his backpack on one side and a cup of hot green tea with a splash of milk and a touch of honey on the other. He had a newspaper on his lap that he pretended to read. Just then he spotted Grace as she exited the building, saw her purchase a cup of coffee from the kiosk, and seat herself on a bench facing Thomas but on the other side of the small park. She set a large purse beside her and subtly peeled down a leather flap on the front, exposing a small dish well inside the open bag.

Thomas unzipped the top of his backpack and laid it down on the bench so that the opened top faced Grace in the distance. He reached in, flipped on the listening device, and put in his ear buds.

Pretending to read his paper, he said in a low voice, "What's a pretty girl like you doing in a place like this?"

Glancing up, he saw Grace over sixty yards away appearing to talk on a cell phone. Her voice suddenly sounded in his ear buds. "I'm here looking for a good-looking guy, but since I don't see one, I guess I'll have to talk to you."

Her words caused Thomas to choke on his tea. "I don't have to put up with this abuse," Thomas returned with a grin, still looking at his paper. "Deputy Trask would be happy to talk with me."

"He thinks you're weird."

"No...no, he doesn't," Thomas corrected. "He thinks I'm strange. There's a big difference."

"There is?"

"Absolutely," Thomas returned. "Weird is just...uh...weird, but strange is socially acceptable."

"Well, Mr. Socially Acceptable Strange Man, have you had any sudden urges lately to stick a knife in someone?"

"You'll be glad to know that, since our last talk, I have given up murder and hatred altogether. I have determined that there's no future in it."

"Wow!" Grace returned. "Maybe you are becoming socially acceptable."

"Seriously, Grace, I pray for Trask every day! What's really bizarre is that I mean it! It's the strangest thing. I went from hating him so much that I wanted to kill him to staying awake at night because I'm concerned over his soul."

"That is what God's grace can do," she answered.

"It's hard to believe I got so far off track, Grace! I'm still not sure how I let hatred get such a grip on my heart in the first place."

"God's goal for each of us is to become like Jesus," she began. "That is what Jesus prayed for in John seventeen, and Peter also talked about it in Second Peter chapter one."

Thomas quickly jotted the verses down on the edge of the paper on his lap.

"All the hatred," Grace continued, "definitely came from bad thinking, bad decisions, and mistakes that you made from your old sinful nature, but the beautiful thing is that God has used those bad choices to make you more like Christ.

"I was reading about it this morning in Philippians chapter one, verse six. It says, *He who began a good work in you will be faithful to complete it.*

"God started this good work in you, Thomas, and is using the circumstances of your life to draw you closer to Himself and to bring you to stronger faith in His Son, Jesus Christ."

"But I messed up," Thomas interjected, "really badly."

"Yes, you did," Grace answered. "But God never gave up on you. He is so loving, powerful, and faithful that, even when we give in to Satan, God still uses our sinful decisions and worldly mistakes to bring us back to Himself and to accomplish His will in our lives.

"Our sins and failures do not define who we are to God. Your Heavenly Father forgave your sins—past, present, and future—through the sacrifice of His Son on the cross when you trusted in Christ as your Savior and began responding in faith to His lordship over your life. That forgiveness is called justification, and it happens instantly. But there's another process from God going on in your life as well. It's called sanctification. It's where God takes your old sinful

261

nature and slowly changes it to become like Jesus. That process takes a lifetime."

"You mean this kind of stuff is going to keep happening to me?" Thomas asked anxiously.

"It happens to all of us," Grace answered, "because God loves us. He doesn't want us to go through the destruction that following the old sinful self brings. That means He's going to give you plenty of opportunities in your life to face and reject Satan's desires for you and to choose God's. But don't worry about it. Just keep saying *yes* to Jesus, and it will all work out fine."

"But what if I don't?" Thomas shot back with concern.

"You may not," Grace answered, "but so what? You didn't say *yes* to Jesus at first this time, and God didn't abandon you, did He?"

"No, He absolutely did not abandon me."

"Thomas," Grace asked, "do you remember what Jesus said during the last supper when He told His disciples that they were about to abandon Him? He didn't rebuke them, condemn them, or even tell them that He was getting new disciples. He said, *Let not your hearts be troubled; believe in God, believe also in Me.*[22] He is *always* on your side, Thomas. He will *always* be there to bring you back to Him if that's what you need."

"Wow!" Thomas exclaimed as he reflected on Grace's words. Tears began to flow down his cheeks again as he said, "Jesus is an awesome Savior and Lord. His love and grace are absolutely amazing!"

---

[22] John 14: 1

"Oops, I'm being paged," Grace interrupted. "Sorry, Thomas. I've got to go back to work. But this has been a nice first date."

"Second date," Thomas corrected. "The first one was at the coffee shop. It just didn't last very long."

"Okay, second date," Grace agreed. "We'd better not meet like this too often, but I'd like to do it again."

"Yeah, me too," Thomas agreed. "How about the day after tomorrow? Same time...same place?"

Even from nearly seventy yards away, Thomas could see the smile on Grace's face as she closed up her purse and picked up her coffee. She was still smiling when she stood up and looked at him from across the park. From his ear buds Thomas heard the beautiful words, "It's a date!"

The End

Appendix

A good story not only entertains you, it should also challenge you to be a better person and make you think higher thoughts. God our Father in the Old Testament and Jesus Christ in the New Testament both used stories to teach important spiritual lessons. It has been discovered that whenever an engaging story is used to instruct, the lessons bypass the short term memory, and go straight to the hippocampus in the brain, where long term memory occurs. By using exciting stories, teachers have the potential to place the lessons directly into the long term memories of their students.

For this reason I want to encourage readers to consider using my stories to teach. To do that I am including chapter questions in this appendix to assist in promoting meaningful discussions. These questions are just suggestions. You may be able to think of some better ones or questions that better fit your group. It is not important to cover all the questions. The important part is to encourage each other to know Christ better, to draw near to God, and to follow Christ more effectively through your discussions.

Find out more about using stories to teach at *www.StoriesChangeHearts.com*

Chapter One

Why is it important to show respect to older people?

What harm does it cause to you and to others when you disrespect people?

When you are upset with someone you are close to how is the best way to handle it?

Explain why letting your emotions rule your words and behaviors is generally harmful.

Why are some people willing to go to prison or die for their faith in Jesus?

List some poor character qualities Mike and his friends demonstrated in this chapter.

Chapter Two

What was Jesus Christ worth to Mike's parents?

How does someone acquire that kind of commitment to Jesus? (What must be embraced and what must be rejected?)

What was Aunt Faye risking to help Mike and why was she risking it?

As Mike panicked about the police raid, what good character qualities did Faye show?

Even though they were in jail, in what ways did Mike's parents help in their son's escape?

<u>Chapter Three</u>

How would it change your thinking or behavior to be under the constant threat of persecution?

It has been shown that churches grow during persecution. Why do you think that is?

If you are a believer, how do you think persecution would affect your faith?

What does God's word say about persecution? (*John 15:19-20, II Timothy 3:11-12, Matthew 5:10-12, I Peter 4:12-14*)

If we are not being persecuted what is our responsibility to those who are? (*Hebrews 13:3*)

How did Jesus respond to persecution?

<u>Chapter Four</u>

What would it be like to have to run and hide from government agents who were trying to track you down?

For Thomas to be successful in avoiding capture what character qualities will he need?

Describe what the people are like who are helping Thomas? What is their motivation?

In what countries does the persecution of Christians happen today?

Have you ever been persecuted for your faith?

<u>Chapter Five</u>

How important was it for Thomas to have help?

What motivates a person to risk death or imprisonment just to help someone else?

How do you think it feels to be in serious trouble and have someone volunteer to help you?

Are you living for a higher purpose than for yourself, and if so, what is it?

What is a person like whose primary purpose in life is to serve themselves?

When Thomas asked Mr. Smith why Jesus was worth risking imprisonment or death for, what did he say?

Chapter Six

If you suddenly had to create a new life for yourself, what decisions would you want to be sure you made?

If you've been saved, what do you owe to God? How should you live your life?

What is the difference between living for yourself and living for a higher purpose?

Do you have a higher purpose that you are living for?

Have you ever asked God who He has called you to be?

Has God told you what your identity is in Christ?

Chapter Seven

What is a house church and how do you think they work?

Why do the followers of Jesus in most persecuted countries rely on house churches?

Where are house churches mentioned in scripture? (*Acts 2:46, 12:12, 16:40; Romans 16:3-5; I Corinthians 16:19; Colossians 4:15; Philemon verses 1-2*)

If you knew for a fact that persecution was coming to you and your family what would you do to prepare?

Jesus told His followers to 'be wise as serpents and as harmless as doves' (*Matthew 10: 16*). Why is this a good description of the Christians you met in this chapter?

Chapter Eight

In John 6:44 Jesus said, "No one can come to the Father unless the Father Who sent Me draws him." In the story, what ways have you noticed God drawing Thomas to Himself?

How has God drawn you to Himself? Describe your spiritual journey.

How does God use blessings, successes, hard times, or trials in a person's life to draw them to Him?

In his prayer, Thomas wrestled with the cost of following Jesus Christ. Explain that cost.

If salvation is a free gift, explain why there is a cost to following Jesus.

<u>Chapter Nine</u>

How did God use Egg's limitations to direct his life?

Are there limitations or weaknesses in your life that God may be using to direct you?

How were Thomas and the girl able to fool any onlookers as to why they were actually meeting?

What good character qualities did Thomas and the girl show in conducting their secret meeting?

When is it a good thing to keep secrets?

Describe some times in the Bible when people of God needed to keep secrets. (*I Samuel 16:1-13, Luke 8:52-56*)

<u>Chapter Ten</u>

When things don't go the way you expect or plan, what is the best way to handle that situation?

How does anger and frustration get in the way of problem solving?

What good character qualities are needed to solve difficult problems?

Because Satan controls much that goes on in our world, Christians are actually living behind enemy lines. With that in mind, what do you think the Bible means when it says that we are to be in the world but not of the world?

Has God ever used you in one of His 'covert operations'?

Chapter Eleven

Is it right or wrong to listen in on peoples conversations?

As one of God's agents why might Thomas need to listen to others?

When God's word says that Christ's followers are to wise as serpents and as harmless as doves, how could that play out in your life?

What are some ways that Jesus hid what He was doing from the Romans and Jewish religious leaders?

Why did Jesus keep some of His work secret?

Chapter Twelve

What godly character qualities is Thomas showing in helping the poor family?

How is Christ revealing Himself in the lives of those who are a part of Thomas's plan?

What are some of the blessings that come to a person when they go out of their way to help others?

Why did Thomas not want the woman and her son to know who was doing this for them?

Chapter Thirteen

Describe some of the things Grace would have to think about daily to avoid being discovered as a spy for the Christian underground.

What would motivate a person to risk so much to do this work?

How important is it for a follower of Jesus to have a good reputation with unbelievers?

How does a follower of Jesus acquire a good reputation with others?

If someone asks you to do something for them, how is the wisest way to handle those requests?

Chapter Fourteen

What is O.J.'s view of the secret work they are doing?

What evidence is there to show that he has put a lot of thought and work in what he's doing for Jesus?

What good character qualities are you seeing in O.J.?

How precious is the Word of God to believers who are living under persecution?

How important should the Word of God be to you?

Chapter Fifteen

What risks were involved in the work Grace and O.J. were doing?

Why would Grace say that the effort was worth the risk?

How do followers of Jesus get the word of God into closed nations today? Is it dangerous to do that?

What is involved in translating the Bible into the different languages of the world today?

Chapter Sixteen

Why is it wise to plan for disaster?

How do you plan for disaster?

What effort and character qualities are needed for emergency plans to be properly implemented?

If you were Grace, what are the first things you would do to prepare for being discovered by the police?

What attitudes do you think God wants you to have when facing relentless persecution?

If persecution comes what do you think is the most important thing to keep in mind?

<u>Chapter Seventeen</u>

Why do Christians under persecution risk so much to get together with other believers?

What does the Bible say about followers of Jesus meeting together? (*Hebrews 10:25, Acts 2:42-47*)

Why do you think God allows persecution to occur? What are some good or beneficial things that come from persecution?

What are some of the promises that God makes to those who are suffering for Him? (*Proverbs 3:3-6, I Corinthians 10:13, II Thessalonians 1:6-8; 3:3, Revelation 2:10*)

Chapter Eighteen

How was Jesus working in this chapter? ...In Dr. Robertson? ...In Thomas? ...In the lady harboring the hiding Christians?

What character qualities did Thomas show in this chapter?

What needs, help, or support would the Christians have who were hiding from the secret police?

How would living under persecution like this affect your faith in God?

Chapter Nineteen

What are some important character qualities to have to be successful at your job?

What poor character qualities did Thomas show to his friends who were concerned about him?

For a person to live a successful life list the priorities they should have, in their proper order.

Thomas's life is sometimes stressful and demanding. How does God want His followers to handle those difficult times?

How does faith in God and knowing God's word help in times of stress?

Chapter Twenty

What character attributes is Thomas showing in this chapter that are important for the work he's doing for God?

When he couldn't find the believers in the park how did Thomas warn them?

Describe what it means to have courage. (Is courage the lack of fear?)

When does God expect his followers to show courage?

Describe some times when Jesus showed courage?

When did some of Jesus' disciples have to be courageous?

Chapter Twenty-One

How would you describe the character of Devlin Trask?

List some of the consequences of living a life like Trask's. How would it affect your relationships?

Describe Trask's god.

What are you learning about Grace's character?

What do you think motivates her to risk her life to be a spy?

Chapter Twenty-Two

What good character qualities can be seen in Danita Jefferson?

What bad character qualities does she display?

Have there been times in your life when you rejected God's direction for your life? What were the consequences of your choices?

Are there times when you have followed God's direction for your life's choices? What were the results?

Why is pride a dangerous attribute for anyone desiring to serve God?

Chapter Twenty-Three

Explain why believers in other areas would risk their lives to come to Grantham to encourage the persecuted believers?

How does God want believers to feel toward Christians who are being persecuted? (*Hebrews 13:3*)

What character qualities are needed for a person to do hard things?

Why is it important to be willing to do hard things, especially for God?

Appendix

Chapter Twenty-Four

What character qualities did Thomas show in getting his message to Mike?

How was Thomas able to answer all of the woman's questions without lying to her?

How did Thomas show wisdom in his interactions with the woman?

In a situation like this what would be the costs of being foolish or careless in your words or behavior?

Who would suffer if you are foolish or careless in your words or behavior?

Chapter Twenty-Five

What godly character qualities are Thomas and Mike going to need to protect two secret guests rather than one?

Do you think Silas' plan to record the information about the persecuted believers is wise or not? (Justify your answer.)

Why was Mike concerned about Silas' notebook? Can you think of a better or safer way to document the important events?

Did you see Jesus at work in anyone in this chapter?

Chapter Twenty-Six

How did Thomas show responsibility in protecting the two men?

How did Thomas show wisdom in this chapter?

Why is Thomas risking his life to protect the others?

How do you explain the difference in Thomas at the beginning of the story and Thomas now?

Chapter Twenty-Seven

Why do you think worshiping God together was so important to the persecuted believers?

How important should worshiping God be to us?

What happens to a person when they genuinely worship God?

What did Paul mean in Acts 14:22 when he said "Through many tribulations we must enter the Kingdom of God"? How is that true for our lives as believers?

When you experience hard times why are God's promises so important for believers?

Chapter Twenty-Eight

Thomas feels guilty for letting the two ministers get caught by the police. Is there anything he could have done differently to prevent that?

How does God want His people to respond when bad things happen?

Sometimes we ask God to do something for us and it doesn't happen. Does that mean God failed, or that He has rejected us?

When faced with a serious challenge what are the things you should do and not do to arrive at the right solution?

Chapter Twenty-Nine

How would you describe O.G.P as a person?

List some of her most noteworthy character qualities?

What sacrifices has she made?

Why would someone do what she does?

What sacrifices have you made for Jesus?

What sacrifices did Jesus make for you?

Chapter Thirty

Why do you think Thomas wanted Linda to read the book of John first?

Danita got frustrated not being able to get the information she needed from Thomas. How is the best way to handle frustration?

Describe a situation that frustrated you. How did you handle it? How should you have handled it?

When tragedy strikes your life what are some good and healthy ways to respond to the grief?

Chapter Thirty-One

If the miracles are so hard to believe why do you think God included them in the Bible?

Can you believe in Jesus and reject the miracles and what Jesus said about Himself?

Jesus claimed to be the Son of God. If you don't believe that to be true then what are you saying about Jesus?

What is confusing about using the term "Christian"?

What are some important reasons to be a follower of Jesus?

Chapter Thirty-Two

When you make plans to serve God how can you be sure they're God's plans instead of yours?

How important is prayer in making plans?

Joshua in the Bible made plans and decisions without checking with God first. What was the result? (*Joshua chapter 9*)

What bad character is Danita showing?

How would you describe Trask's character?

Chapter Thirty-Three

Describe what is happening to Danita.

Why do you think Danita is allowing God to work in her life now?

What good character is she now showing?

How did Jesus show Himself in this chapter?

How has Jesus revealed Himself in your life? Can others see Jesus in you?

Chapter Thirty-Four

Describe the character qualities needed by all the ones willing to slip into the jail to rescue their friends.

How does a person acquire the courage and the motivation to risk your life for others?

Why did Jesus do what He did for us?

How does God communicate His will to us in our day to day lives?

Discuss why it is important to God that you be alive at this time in history.

Chapter Thirty-Five

What does bitterness and unforgiveness do to a person?

Have you ever experienced this?

What does God say we can expect if we are unwilling to forgive those who have offended us? (*Matthew 6:12, 15; 18:21-35*)

What has to happen within a person in order to genuinely forgive someone?

When you forgive someone does that mean that there are no longer any consequences for their offence? Explain.

___

Chapter Thirty-Six

The Bible says that it's not a sin to be angry, but how can anger turn into wrath and hatred?

When does anger become sin?

What effect does hatred have on the person who hates?

How does Jesus help a person be free of hatred and bitterness?

What should it mean to us when the Bible says, 'Vengeance is mine, says the Lord'?

How did Jesus respond when He was betrayed, tortured, and murdered?

___

Chapter Thirty-Seven

How does a person allow Satan to control parts of their heart?

What must we do when we realize Satan is influencing us?

Why is it good to confess our sins to others?

What are some of the benefits of talking over problems and concerns with mature believers?

How is God accomplishing Philippians 1: 6 in your life? Can you give some examples?

Chapter Thirty-Eight

Why is it important to be persistent in our prayers? (*Luke 18:1-8*) Can you give some examples of believers who were persistent in prayer?

What is to be our response to sinners even if they have not repented? (*I Timothy 2:1-4, Matthew 18:15-18*)

What is to be our response to sinners after they repent? (*II Corinthians 2:5-8*)

Why are we to be patient with others who are struggling with sin? (*Galatians 6:1*)

What should Thomas do to protect himself and prepare for future temptations?

<u>Chapter Thirty-Nine</u>

How did Thomas and Grace show creativity in conducting their counseling session?

How do you explain the changes in how Thomas views Trask now?

What happens in a person's heart when they genuinely pray for their enemies?

How easy is it for Satan to distract us from God's purposes for us?

How should we use trusting in God's promises to keep Satan's attacks from harming us?

If our sins and failures are not to define who we are, what does define who we are?

Who does God say that you are?

About the Author

Alan W. Harris is a retired veterinarian who lives near Luray, Virginia, where he and Valerie, his wife of nearly fifty years, make their home. They have six children whom they homeschooled for twenty-seven years, a growing host of beautiful grandchildren, whom they adore,...and a pug.

Alan's motivation to write sprang from a desire to share an exciting story with his children. He wanted to not just entertain them, but to teach them important character and spiritual lessons. The tale needed to be very suspenseful, and the characters had to be engaging and fun in order to keep his children interested. The results were *The Tales of Larkin* series, which has five books. You can find out more about them as well as how to use them to teach at **StoriesChangeHearts.com**.

In searching for other subjects about which to write, Alan came up with *The Flintlock Sagas* series, which to date contains three books.

His book, <u>The Other Side of the Veil</u>, is written more for adults and is meant not only to tell an interesting story, but also to challenge the reader to consider their everlasting future as well as God's will and His work in their lives on this side of the eternity.

It is Alan's prayer that his new book, <u>Thomas Westcott: God's Shadow Agent</u>, will not only entertain his readers, but also help them grow in godly character and move them to take their walk with God the Father and His Son, King Jesus to a deeper and more devoted level.

Other Works by Alan W. Harris
*(Find out more at **StoriesChangeHearts.com**)*

The Tales of Larkin

Book 1 **Hawthorn's Discovery** - Hawthorn's Discovery is a non-stop Christian adventure story of one inch tall woodland warriors. Full of fast-paced action, suspense and humor, this tale of deliverance is fun for the whole family.

Book 2 **Larkin's Journal** - This second book in the series is the prequel to book one and reveals the history of these tiny people. The story is of Larkin, son of Ramus, who will eventually become the patriarch of all of the Larkin tribes. From an early age Larkin's life is filled with adventure, danger, and intrigue; and he finds a loving Lord along the way.

Book 3 **The Great Gathering** - This story starts two years after Hawthorn and his friends in book one return from their secret exploits with the Makerian people. They are recruited to join a covert plan to bring the knowledge of the Maker's love to all the Larkin clans. The friends soon learn that following the King sometimes exacts a high cost. This book starts with a rush and continues with rapid-fire action and meaningful spiritual insights.

Book 4 **Mosstar and Belladonna** - This story takes place one hundred and fifty years in the Larkin's past. Not only must princess Belladonna and the tree laird's son survive frequent life-threatening dangers but they must face the Maker's truth about their own lives. Unknown to them is a diabolical plot to destroy them both and forever change the Larkin's future.

Book 5 **Fiery Trials** - This picks up the continuing story of Hawthorn and his friends. Two years have passed since the end of book three and the jealous Shaman have an opportunity to finally destroy the followers of Jehesus. Devastating disease and an unimaginable disaster must be faced if the King's followers are to survive.

The Flintlock Sagas

Book 1 **The Young Frontiersman** - Young William Hackett is a part of a group of pioneers starting a new life in the wilderness of Kentucky in the 1770's. They share constant peril, as well as facing the threat of attack by native warriors stirred up by British agents. Set during the Revolutionary War the exciting story demonstrates God's faithfulness to us, whether the battles we face are against physical enemies or spiritual ones.

Book 2 **The Maker's Medicine Girl** - No one knew the dangers of the Kentucky wilderness better than sixteen year old Remember Warren. Her village burned and her family and friends violently murdered by Indians, the girl found herself a slave of a renegade trapper and his Shawnee squaw. Though she doesn't believe it, God has not forsaken her. Will she look beyond the hardship and listen to God's higher purpose for all her suffering? The story reaches its climax as Ember is forced to make a desperate run for her life that will put her new faith to the extreme test.

Book 3 **The Dancing Ghosts** - Discovering the ghost-like figures dancing among the trees was enough to seriously concern Asa Whitlock and the two women with him. Then after the dancers tried to kill them as they raced back to Larkinboro, the town leaders knew they needed to know what was going on. Will Hackett, Grey Fox, Dirt Gurley, and Asa were sent to determine what these strange enemies were up to, but the more they learned the more terrifying the situation became. Eventually they must trust God and risk their lives to save their families, friends and even the

American troops sent to defend them. Full of fast paced adventure, humor, and the faithfulness of God, this book will be hard to put down.

The Other Side of the Veil

An adult Christian fiction story.

A victim of a plane crash, Blake Miller finds his conscious self in a terrifying near death experience. When he is chased by demons and threatened with hideous torture, Blake's world is changed when he discovers that his only hope of escape lies with two angels sent because of his grandmother's prayers.

Milton Collins, a new follower of Jesus, dies in the same crash and is amazed at the discoveries of Paradise. Stunned by the beauty and love he experiences there, Milton seeks to find a way to help those he left behind. The horrors of hell are starkly contrasted with the glories of Paradise in this gripping story of events on the other side of the veil.

Keep up with Alan Harris, his short stories about the life of Jesus taken from the Gospel of John, *The Other Side of the Veil, The Flintlock Sagas,* and his first series, *The Tales of Larkin,* as well as learning how to use stories to teach to the hearts of your children or students at **www.StoriesChangeHearts.com**.

If you wish to contact Alan you can e-mail him at **StoriesChangeHearts@gmail.com**.

www.ingramcontent.com/pod-product-compliance
Lightning Source LLC
Chambersburg PA
CBHW060534180626
46817CB00002B/562